unravelling his MARK

ZEE MONODEE

ACKNOWLEDGEMENTS

This book wouldn't have been possible without the vision Kiru Taye had of The Protectors' series—she planted that niggling little idea in my head, and the result is this story. I have to thank her for giving me this opportunity and also for all she is doing for Africa, it romance, and its authors.

Further thanks go to the beta readers who helped me out when I finished this story: Natalie G. Owens, Chicki Brown, Razia Sultana, Joanna Torreano, & Mandy Verbaan. You ladies were awesome!

Last but not least, thanks to the Universe, for always having my back.

DEDICATION

For my beloved dad—for all he did and still does for me even though he is no longer of this world.

CHAPTER ONE

Kinshasa, Democratic Republic of Congo
Thursday, January 29. 10.42 p.m.

"Damn it! Don't die on me! Don't you dare die on me, Vosloo!"

Zachariah 'Zach' Hashemi fell to his knees beside the prone body of Dax Vosloo. A bullet whizzed past his head less than a second later. He ducked, flattened himself to the dirty floor, and dragged his companion with him behind a solid wall after making sure there were no openings on this side of the abandoned building. There was no time to retaliate, not when a sniper had his lens trained on them.

The bullets kept coming, raining shards of concrete into the air. They didn't pierce the wall, though, which already gave him an idea of the calibre used. This was probably not from a military-grade rifle—their .50BMG, .338 Lapua Magnum, or .300 Winchester Magnum rounds would've caused way more collateral damage.

No, this was probably from a semi-auto sniper platform. Whoever was after them had to be some low-life mercenary or the like, but this person wasn't the one they had come here looking for. This was too crude, too unpolished.

The stealthy assassin known in their circles as Evangeline did everything with elegance and class. This shit show here couldn't be her work.

Or could it—because the target had clearly been Vosloo: the killer's former associate, the only one who knew her true identity. Vosloo might've been getting too close, thus the need to remove him from the board by any means.

Silence descended on the premises, broken by the gurgled spurts coming from Vosloo's throat.

Zach got up onto his knees and pushed aside the other man's shirt to ascertain the damage the bullet had wrought.

A gaping wound bled on his left shoulder.

Damn it. The shooter had hit centre mass, just low enough to cause irreparable damage to the blood flow network around the heart and lungs. Vosloo wouldn't survive this.

"Tell me," he growled as he shook the man to keep him awake. "Who is Evangeline?"

Vosloo seemed to be zoning out.

He couldn't let him die without telling them who the woman was. Vosloo was their only lead.

"For once in your shitty life, you son of a bitch, do the right thing! Tell me who Evangeline is!"

Vosloo's rheumy green eyes grew wide. He must have seen death coming for him. The man had always been a coward.

"Anna …" he mumbled.

"What?" Zach lowered his head closer to Vosloo's face so he could hear the words.

"Annabwe … Viarbe."

Zach blinked. This was utter gibberish. "You're not making much sense, man. Come on, hang on. Tell me—"

"Annab—" Vosloo's head fell onto his shoulder, his eyes glassy and open.

He was dead.

"Damn it!"

Zach stood and kicked the wall in frustration.

They'd come here because they'd heard another associate of Evangeline operated out of this hijacked building in the Congolese capital. The person handled the communications network allowing her to conduct her kills without care or concern that she could get caught. A Kali—as such female assassins were known inside the Corpus, the clandestine agency he worked for—relied on a criminal facilitator to carry off her measles operations—assassinations leaving no trace of a killer's involvement. Evangeline had never really been one of theirs, though, even if she had tried her darned best.

Dax Vosloo had been Evangeline's lover before both their trails had gone cold about a year earlier. The man had, however, turned himself in to Corpus a few weeks before, working with them to unravel the killer's network. He had so far sent them on a wild goose chase that had unearthed 'intel' but still no clue as to who the woman was.

Until now. Could those mumbled words actually mean something?

It was the only lead they had, though. Vosloo was dead.

By this point, the bullets had definitely stopped raining, and with the wall behind his back, Zach could stay put for a long time. It sucked, but he could do it. With a sigh, he pulled out his cell phone and tapped in a number. It rang twice on the other end, then an operator picked up. Instead of replying, he entered a sequence of numbers and cut the call.

Seconds later, the phone vibrated in his palm. He picked up, knowing his boss would be calling after having been given the message implied in the code.

"He's dead," he said without preamble.

"Shit," the woman at the other end cursed. "Did he say anything?"

"Annabwe and viarbe."

"It was her?"

She hadn't said anything about those words not making sense. She wouldn't pronounce herself on that until she was sure they really didn't mean anything.

"Negative."

She remained silent for a few seconds. "Come back to Berlin ASAP. I'll have them ready the plane for you at the airstrip."

Berlin? Not Prague, as per the usual procedure?

Over this connection, they could talk without fear of being listened to. A network of proxy servers rerouted the call locations, hence the practice of calling a central switchboard and the operator then directing the requests. The calls happened across the same encrypted net connecting the entire Corpus framework through its hyper-tight security protocols.

She cut the call; he'd been dismissed.

With a final look at Vosloo's dead body, he crouched low and pulled out his Heckler & Koch P30 semi-automatic pistol. The shooter might still be around even if the bullets had stopped raining. Though he doubted that. The target had been despatched, and Zach wasn't to be collateral—he would be dead already if his name had been on the brief. Whoever had done this had wanted just Vosloo out of the picture.

His mind told him it had to be Evangeline, but something felt off about it. It also couldn't be her. She loved to go for the slow kill, the more twisted and psychopathic the better. This had been too straightforward to be her work.

Maybe his boss would have some answers for him.

His steps careful and measured, he made his way out of the building, crouching around openings. He sure would not offer himself up as a moving target now.

***

Berlin, Germany. Potsdamer Platz corporate district Friday, January 30. 11.24 a.m.

Zach took the lift inside the *Dynamogenics* headquarters building. The doors opened onto the carpeted inner sanctum of the company located on the top floor of the tower. His long strides took him across the massive space.

Vero, the boss' PA and also her bodyguard, looked up from her desk and gave him a small smile. He returned the smile and added a nod. She cocked her head towards the wide mahogany doors to the side.

Nobody seeing them here would imagine the two of them had spent a wild night burning the sheets of his bed inside the company accommodations in Djibouti a little while ago.

Blonde Vero who looked deceptively like an innocent and wholesome girl-next-door had been sent to establish a satellite office of tech and R&D giant

Dynamogenics there. But this was actually a cover for having Corpus agents on the ground in the African city that had become the centre of the spy game on the continent, like what Berlin had been during the Cold War.

They'd spent the one night together, then she had come back here, and he'd stayed over, positioned there under the cover of being the security consultant for the whole office. She'd moved on, he'd moved on—and that's how it should be. There was no place for emotional entanglements and even attachment in their world. He'd closed the door on the thought of love a long time ago.

The thick door opened to let him into a bright and airy office, the floor-to-ceiling windows at the far end revealing a panorama of Berlin, Brandenburg Gate distinctly visible in the distance. Behind the massive desk sat a redhead who many would describe as an alabaster bridal mannequin come to life. The world knew Alexis Friedrich as the daughter of the late Tobias Friedrich who'd founded *Dynamogenics* during the Cold War. She handled her CEO duties with panache and played the slightly ditzy heiress in social circles with flair.

Only a select few were aware she had also inherited the clandestine Corpus Agency from her father, at the head of all its operations now.

Zach's gaze slid from her to the older man with the swept-back dark hair and the large black-framed glasses on his patrician nose. He frowned. What was Simon Wexler doing here? The guy was the founder of Wexler-Prinsloo, the most prominent communications and ad agency in the whole African region. Yet another front for Corpus.

"Zachariah," Alexis said, nodding towards the empty sofa beside Wexler.

She was the only one who never made use of his moniker. It always felt off to hear himself being called by his full name. Even his father used the shortened Zach.

"Ma'am." He took his seat after undoing the button on his suit jacket.

She joined them on the three-seater across. "You're sure it wasn't Evangeline?"

"Yes. The facts don't add up. Nobody knew we were going to be there. Vosloo wouldn't have let it leak, knowing he would easily become a target. Believe me, the man was too much of a coward to face such danger willingly."

"You say he arranged the meet?"

"He'd found the network's engineer would be on site that night. It wasn't even a meet, since this was supposed to be a surprise landing on the target."

"Someone must've been following you," she said.

Zach nodded. "My theory, too. But it wasn't Evangeline. An associate, or a gun for hire, but not her."

Alexis simply lifted an eyebrow in question.

"Well, firstly, the strike was way too messy to be hers. She's a narcissist, loves to leave her signature on her kills. Knowing her, if she'd even gone for a long-range gun, it would've been a single headshot neatly in the middle of the forehead using a hollow-point bullet like a Black Talon that would've torn his brain apart but contained the shot inside his cranium. No exit wound, no blood and gore splatter. Elegant and almost poetic, even. Vosloo was killed by a 7.62x51 rifle bullet." He paused at the confusion on Wexler's face. "Civilians know it as .308 calibre. Way too common for her tastes. I didn't find the sniper's nest; the person would've already fled from the site by the time I got out, but the closest building offering such range was three blocks from where we were. She likes to get as close as possible for her kills."

"Hmm," Alexis hummed.

When she remained silent, Zach started to get up. The debriefing must be over. He'd been surprised she'd even asked him here. Alexis oversaw all operations, but the nitty gritty was handled by her second in command, Graeme, over at The Retreat, their covert facility in north-western Prague.

But Evangeline seemed to be a sore spot with the big boss. From what Zach had gathered, Alexis' biological mother had tried a coup on the agency, which had resulted in a mutiny inside the ranks and the murder of her father. Evangeline had been the woman's designated assassin, the Kali—the harbinger of death, the bringer of destruction. She was the only loose thread left to apprehend from that mutinous uprising.

"You also gave us some intel," she continued without even looking at him.

They weren't done. He sat back down.

"Yes. Vosloo said two words. Annabwe and viarbe."

He didn't ask if she'd figured out what they meant. She would tell him if she wanted him in the loop.

She pressed a small fob in her hand, and the big screen on the wall across from them came on. A slideshow started, pictures of the same woman. A brunette, White, with thick, long black hair, delicate features on a tiny face with fragile bones, and gunmetal grey eyes slightly upturned at the outer corners, suggesting she might have some Asian blood in her lineage. The first image looked like a professional headshot. The others were candid snaps of her always in classy clothing as she went about her day. One picture was of her in a bikini as she prepared to dive into a pool.

A beautiful woman, for sure. Late twenties, he'd say.

He blinked. "Wait. Is that ...?"

"Evangeline?" Alexis asked. "She might be."

Zach blinked. This creature looked like ... an angel. She couldn't be a stone-hearted killer. Her blinding smile in the headshot picture?

Unless she used it as a façade to lure everyone. He was a spy—he of all people should know the face people presented to the world sometimes had nothing to do with what they really were inside.

A shiver coursed through him. "Who is she?"

Alexis nodded at the other man, who had remained silent so far. "Simon?"

Simon Wexler cleared his throat and waved his hand at the screen. "This woman is, officially, Annabelle de Castelban ..."

Annabwe ... Could Vosloo have been saying Annabelle?

"... Thirty-four-year-old French-Mauritian who owns and heads a boutique communications and events management agency called Sparkle Communications on the island. The agency also has an ad and design leg called Glitter Ads. Comes from an illustrious family who is still a big landowner in Mauritius."

"What makes you think she is Evangeline?" he asked.

Alexis spoke this time. "She is also Dax Vosloo's ex-girlfriend. Whenever there has been an Evangeline kill before December of the previous year, both Dax and

Annabelle have been in the country of the hit in the same period. It might be a coincidence, but I don't like to dismiss such occurrences."

The gears inside Zach's brain were clicking together fast. "And in the past year, since both Evangeline and Vosloo went dark ..."

"She has remained in Mauritius, yes," Simon continued. "With a trip once to Grenoble to visit her mother, she hasn't left the country otherwise. We have no intel of any hit carried out in France around that region or in that period, though."

They wouldn't be telling him all this if they didn't want him on board this operation, whatever it turned out to be. So he pressed on.

"And *viarbe*? You found out what it could mean?"

Alexis shook her head. "No clue. We're hoping Ms. de Castelban could know."

And how would they— Of course. "I'm going to Mauritius?"

"You are. Simon will be able to tell you more."

He turned his attention onto Simon Wexler.

"Your file says you completed your MBA with scores in the ninety-to-one-hundred range."

Zach nodded. "I did."

Fat lot of good it had done him in the military, though. He'd gone to business school to please his father and also to be close to home while his sister finished her secondary schooling. But sitting behind a desk crunching numbers and reports had not been his thing. He'd needed the field, the outdoors, better use of his strategizing brain.

"I hope you haven't forgotten all that bull, because you're about to put it to good use," Simon added.

Had the man been reading his mind or what?

"I'm the security consultant for the Djibouti division," Zach stated.

"Not anymore," chimed in Alexis. "For the next two weeks, at least, you'll be considering a career change. Spy work can get tedious, and you are, let us say, weary of it all, so you're looking at other options."

"Like assessing an agency's eligibility to become a Wexler-Prinsloo partner," Simon volleyed.

Zach chuckled and concealed a smile when he figured what they were getting at. "So my cover into Annabelle de Castelban's entourage will be as a Wexler-Prinsloo rep. What's my mission?"

It would be the perfect cover—few outside the Corpus knew of the agency's role as a front. The mutinous group had never targeted the outfit; it must mean they hadn't known of its clandestine purpose.

Alexis didn't blink. "To find out if Annabelle de Castelban is indeed Evangeline and taking the appropriate measures, should it be the case."

In other words, despatch her to kingdom come before she could do more harm.

He trained his gaze onto the screen. Alexis had stopped the slideshow onto the headshot image of Annabelle. The woman had her head slightly tilted to the side, her smile open and beguiling, her pale skin looking creamy and smooth in the black and white shot.

Her eyes, though … They spoke of something else. Of depths. Of darkness.

Of death?

He took in a deep breath. Only one way to find out. "When do I leave?"

***

*Pamplemousses, Mauritius. Château de Venus
Saturday, January 31. 9.14 p.m.*

To Hell in a handbasket. That's where this whole event was going!

Annabelle de Castelban marched backstage at the fashion show like a Fury on crack. If anything went south during this evening, it would reflect badly on her agency, and she could *not* have that. She had worked too hard, invested too much, into Sparkle Communications to have a low-life rat take her down.

Don't play the victim.

The words popped into her mind, and she paused for a second in a dark corner of the hallway to let herself think them through. Leaning against the brushed wood panel covering all the walls in this colonial period dwelling, she closed her eyes and took in a deep breath.

Tonight's fashion gala showcasing up and coming Mauritian designer Nina Harelson hadn't been easy for her to nab. If it hadn't been for Hector Valriche, a family friend of the Harelsons, she would never have been able to establish the connection. Having Hector on as a possible future partner of Sparkle had swayed Nina to give them the deal of organizing her first major fashion show on Mauritian soil. A 'name' already abroad, Nina would thus have press people from Europe, Australia, and the Middle East at this unveiling.

This would've been a significant coup for Sparkle, and having to double-down with Hector on this hadn't seemed like a chore. Hector knew people. As much as Annabelle prided herself on having an extensive contacts list and counting the unofficial social queen of Mauritian society as a good friend, there were still some heights she couldn't touch alone. Of course, she could ask said social queen to introduce her around, but that wouldn't have felt right. Too much like nepotism, which she abhorred.

So why, then, hadn't she put her foot down when Hector had clearly played such a card tonight?

Everything had been arranged; she'd made sure of it. But forty-eight hours before the gala, the little shit had cancelled the catering company Annabelle had worked with for years in favour of his inexperienced niece's start-up.

The prawn cocktail had gone off, and thank goodness her assistant, Daniel, with his super-sensitive sense of smell, had figured something fishy was going on. And she didn't mean that as a pun, either. To cut costs, the idiot niece had actually stirred in fish sauce so the smell would mask the dearth of prawns in the mix. This had made the mayonnaise turn—no wonder, on a night when the temperatures flirted with thirty-five degrees Celsius outside and way higher inside. The air-conditioning was waging a lost battle in these big rooms and such a crush of people.

They'd managed to ditch the spoilt food before it had gone out to be served, though.

If she got her hands on Hector ...

No, she would *not* play the victim. She would own up to her shit, as opposed to some people who never did— *Do* not *think of your mother now!*

Too bad she hadn't put her foot down when he had played the catering switcheroo on her. She'd fucked up, definitely. But she'd make things right, now. Starting with letting Hector go. This partnership would never work.

Of course, he would smear her name once she released him from their verbal agreement, telling the world she was an ungrateful bitch who had dumped him after she'd gotten the event's contract from Nina Harelson. He didn't know she had an ace to counter his strike, though.

Nobody knew of the call from Wexler-Prinsloo the day before.

She'd almost fallen out of her chair when the video call had come in that Friday around ten in the morning. The screen had lit up, and indeed, the image of *the* Simon Wexler had materialized. She had totally recognized the man who looked like a fifty-something Yves Saint Laurent as he was one of her heroes.

What he'd said had floored her. He and John Prinsloo had apparently been keeping an eye on Sparkle, and they were considering the agency to join them as an associate. Someone would be arriving early next week to shadow her for two weeks to see if they had what it took to be a Wexler-Prinsloo partner.

This had come before the debacle of tonight, and had nothing to do with Hector or his helping out. The timeline would speak for her when the bastard started his mud-slinging campaign.

So that was settled. Monday, she would tell Hector they were done. Hopefully before the Wexler-Prinsloo rep came to the office. Then, she and her team would be on their best behaviour for two weeks and totally nab this deal.

With a deep, fortifying breath, she opened her eyes and tore herself from the wall. The stiletto heels on her shoes made clopping sounds as she stalked across the antique teakwood parquets running the length of this château. She paused on the edge of the podium, swathed at the back in the shadows expertly created through the play of lights lighting up the runway. The brilliance hurting her eyes died down somewhat as the last model from the opening line-ups stepped backstage. Nina's collection would come on soon, after a brief intermission.

She had better go check if all was well with the diva.

A mixture of apprehension and unease started roiling inside her stomach the farther in she went. This bade nothing good. She hadn't eaten the prawn cocktail and didn't remember, had she? No, she never ate on big nights. Nerves twisted her too much. She doubted the sparkling water she loved to sip on to keep her electrolytes up would be making her sick today. In fact, it should be helping her stay hydrated amid all this ambient heat.

If everything had been going to Hell in a hand-basket earlier, well, now, all Hell had broken loose.

She stopped dead at the sight of diminutive Nina stomping her feet around and cursing everyone out. They just needed her to start rolling around on the floor for this to be a full-on tantrum.

"You!" Nina shouted when she noticed Annabelle, who cringed at being put on the spot.

Of course, when everything went well during an event, praise went to her whole team. When something—anything—went wrong or sideways, she was singled out to bear the abuse.

"You let this happen," Nina raged on. "Fix this!"

Fix what?

It wouldn't pay to antagonize the client, so she pulled on all the calm and Zen she could conjure and pasted a smile on her face. "Nina, I am sure whatever it is, we can make it right."

"Make it right? How will you? Do you know how long it took me to find him? This show couldn't happen until I found him, and now, he can't do it!"

Who can't do what? She sighed inwardly as Daniel sidled up to her.

"It's not good, *patronne*. The model who was to have the showstopper bride on his arm ate some of the prawn cocktail. He is currently puking his guts out in the guest loo at the back."

"Thank God he made it to the loo and didn't barf on any of the clothes."

Trust her problem-solving mind to come up with the silver lining in every situation. But seriously, if any of the gowns had been ruined, Nina would've had her hide. All the pieces had thousands of pearls or Swarovski crystals hand-sewn on them.

Think, Annabelle, think.

"So the only problem we have right now is that we need an escort for the showstopper."

"And her," Daniel whispered with a glance towards a still-raving Nina.

"Her, we can deal with, and it will sort itself out once we find a replacement for the sick model."

Daniel snorted. "Good luck with that. Have you forgotten the brief she forced down the throat of every modelling agency on the island? The man had to be buff and—"

"Taller than six-foot-two. I know."

Good luck finding a six-foot man at random on the island in the first place, and now on such short notice? They had their work cut out for her.

Still, there were some foreigners in the audience. There must be one about six-two and muscular. What had Nina written on the call sheet? She'd wanted 'a tall drink of water.'

There was no time to ponder the situation. The sooner they calmed Nina down, the sooner they'd get this show underway, and the sooner this night would be over, too.

So, armed with optimism and determination, Annabelle strutted back into the main room, a smile plastered on her face as she eyed every single man around. Just her luck. None seemed taller than six feet, and they all looked like guys whose only attempt at exercise came from a leisurely stroll once a month along a putting green.

Her spirits were sinking fast, but no, she wouldn't be the victim. She would turn this around one way or another. If she couldn't find— Her shoulder collided into someone, and reflex made her look up and say, "*Oh, pardon.*"

But the apology died on her lips as her gaze raked over the hulking piece of masculinity she'd bumped into. He was tall, all right. Comfortably above six-two, she'd say, with the frame to match. Those broad, broad shoulders looked snug inside the clean lines of an obviously expensive hand-tailored suit the shade of a rare *Dom Pérignon millésime*. His skin was the colour of sugar when it had just started to turn into caramel, a golden glow on his chiselled features and cheekbones so sharp and defined, it was ridiculous. His head was shaved, and his eyes were dark. Smouldering. Intense. A thin goatee that looked like it had been hand-drawn onto him framed his solid chin and gave bearing to his strong jaw.

A puff of air escaped her.

"Tall drink of water," she mumbled, and blinked.

The gears of her stunned mind started clicking then, and she gasped. "Tall drink of water!"

The man looked at her with a frown on his broad forehead. He must think she was crazy.

Of course, her words wouldn't make much sense to him. She had enough trouble keeping up with the direction her thoughts had taken.

So she forced herself to pull in a breath, anchored herself solidly on her heels, and threw her shoulders back. She beamed a dazzling smile his way as she psyched herself to give her pitch.

"S'il vous plaît, dites-moi que vous pouvez m'aider!"

She went into her spiel, but a few words in, he shook his head and raised his eyebrows. She stopped talking, and he said, "English, please."

Okay, so definitely a foreigner. A local would understand French.

"So, I need your help. Please, pretty please," she said with another smile.

"Pray tell how."

He had a deep voice with a masculine rumble that almost made her knees go weak. She had a job to do and a crisis to avert here—she couldn't let a man, no matter how delicious-looking, turn her into mush. She'd also picked up the hint of an accent, like a drawl. He actually sounded East African, without the crispness of Francophone Africans.

"Are you averse to being in the spotlight?"

No use beating around the bush.

"Not really. Why?"

His frown seemed to say he was carefully wondering what she might be getting at.

"I will need you for five minutes, tops."

"Doing what?"

She glanced at the ramp, still bathed in low lights, as they waited for the first model wearing Nina's new collection to come out.

"Walking the runway."

He chuckled. "I'm no model."

At least, he hadn't outright refused or told her she was insane. She could work with that.

"You could be, though, with those looks."

He threw his head back and laughed. A few heads turned their way—those people must also have been mesmerized by the rich sound.

"I hear Nina Harelson's designs can be, how shall I put it, out there," he said.

"It's entirely a women's collection," she reassured him.

His eyebrows rose. "You want me to wear a dress? Hmm, kinky."

The way he'd said that last word accompanied by a half-smile almost made her knickers combust. Quickly, she shook herself and got back into the conversation.

"Nah. You'll just have to be, well, you, like this," she said with a wave.

Nina had arranged for the showstopper escort to wear a Cerruti 1881 suit.

"What designer made your outfit?" she asked.

"Hugo Boss."

Perfect. Same parent company representing the two brands along with Christian Lacroix and Ungaro, among others. She could smooth that wrinkle out after the fact.

He eyed the catwalk for long seconds then looked to her. "One turn down there?"

"Yes. That's all I'm asking."

He grinned. "What's in it for me?"

She gulped. Anything he wanted, she would happily give him. Preferably in a moonlit room, with a bed draped in satin sheets. Heck, who needed a mattress? The wall nearby in the darkened hallway would do just fine.

Get your mind out of the gutter, you slut!

"Name your price," she bit out.

He watched her for a moment. "Rain check, for now?"

She gulped again. This would put her at his mercy …

But more important right now was saving this show, stopping a major outburst that would have the reporters in titters backstage, and making sure her agency came out unscathed.

"Deal," she said, and put her hand out.

He clasped it, and the heat flowing into her had nothing to do with the crushing temperatures inside the crowded room.

Priorities, Annabelle. Priorities.

Without releasing his hand, she dragged him out back and into Nina's entourage. Well, non-entourage would be more fitting—everyone seemed to have left that boat to sink, the diva's tantrums being legendary.

"Nina," she soothed as she got close. "Problem solved. Look who I found to step in."

Nina stopped her swearing mid-rant and trained her eagle-eyed, predatory gaze onto the man—wait, she didn't even have a name for him.

"He'll do," the designer said. "He'll do nicely. The suit, though—"

"It's Hugo Boss. They won't have a qualm that it's not the Cerruti 1881 they sent us."

"Perfect. Come with me," Nina said as she grabbed the man's arm in a tight grip.

He turned as she led him away and winked at Annabelle.

"That rain check? I'll find you sometime."

A rush of heat went over her, despite the fact she was standing right under an air-conditioning vent. This amber-skinned Adonis would be the death of her … if this night didn't kill her first.

Figuratively tugging her big girl panties higher, she left the backstage area and went to give the green light to the crew in front that the show could start. Duties snapped her up, like making sure the DJ had his set right and the models were in the proper line-up. She also often darted to the buffet in the main hall to ensure nothing that could be spoilt had stayed on. It was too late to order new catering, though she had managed to ring a nearby hotel and get them to send her a dozen trays of canapés. Consequently, she missed the rest of the show.

By the time she finally had a moment to breathe and look around, the event was over, and her Mystery Man was nowhere to be found.

Chapter Two

Port-Louis, Mauritius. St Georges Street
Monday, February 2. 9.03 a.m.

"Good. Everyone's here. Gather up!"

Annabelle rallied her team close to her in the wide veranda at the front of the restored colonial house that was the head office of Sparkle Communications. Chairs scraped around the big glass and steel table, and, as usual, someone started slapping their ankle because mosquitoes were biting.

She sighed, having no clue how this could keep happening as she had citronella candles burning all around the place. The someone was usually Daniel, with his thin, pale skin. He wanted her to chuck all the potted ferns near the French doors and replace them with plastic ones. Which made her shudder every single time. Daniel might be invaluable to her, but she drew the line at a clean, oxygen-rich workspace free of chemical fumes from those mosquito repellents.

When everyone had settled down, including Deepika, their receptionist, she parked herself at one end of the table but remained standing. This way, she could keep an eye on ze entrance lobby and check for visitors. She needed everyone around when she imparted the news, hence the unmanned front desk.

"Okay, peeps. We'll keep this quick," she started in Creole.

The others had made fun of her accent when they'd just started working together—she was French-Mauritian. Her kind spoke French, generally, and even then, with a distinct accent and lilt setting them clearly apart from native French people. A bit like hearing a Parisian and a French-Canadian from Quebec speak; they'd both be speaking French, able to understand each other, but you'd never say they came from the same world. So French-Mauritians, with their drawling French accent, spoke Creole like that, too, instead of the crisp, sharp intonation with which other Mauritian natives spoke the mother tongue.

"First on the agenda, we will not be continuing our association with Hector Valriche."

"Thank the Lord," someone muttered.

Haseena, their social media manager, had fewer qualms and shot an outright, "*Alhamd'lillah!* The man is creepy."

Annabelle glanced her way and pursed her lips. "Yeah, so you kept saying. I did wake up from whatever spell he had on me, though. Better late than never, right?"

"Exactly," the other woman retorted with a wide smile.

"So, Deeps," she said as she turned to the receptionist. "Get him on the phone and tell him to get his arse here ASAP today."

Deepika made a grimace, but she placed two fingers to her forehead and saluted, giving the non-verbal okay to the request.

"Now, next up, and this is a big one, guys. Who here knows what Wexler-Prinsloo is?"

"Duh, *patronne*. Only the biggest comms agency on the African territory?" Daniel chimed in.

"Exactly," she concurred. "And guess who had Simon Wexler on the other end of her phone recently?"

"No way!" Haseena bellowed.

Annabelle stifled a grimace at the exclamation. With exuberant Haseena around, no one else got to place in a word. The other handful of staff around the table remained silent. Only Daniel had the guts—or enough folly inside him—to go up against her usually.

"Way," she continued. "Simon Wexler says our agency has been on his radar for a while, and they are considering us to become one of their partners."

"Wow, that was fast. We heard nothing before," Haseena said.

Annabelle nodded. "I know. They surprised me, too. But we're not gonna look a gift horse in the mouth, are we? He wants us in with them if we make the cut. I say 'thank God' for the opportunity."

Their name would change to Sparkle Wexler-Prinsloo if this dream came true. They would have access to all the resources of the entire WP network on top of their doors opening wide for even more international and local involvement with such a name and reputation backing them up.

It would be the coup of the century for her.

"So how are they going to ascertain that?" Daniel asked.

Good thing he'd asked—he'd brought her back to the here and now from her visualizations of their perfect future.

"They're sending someone who should be coming in this week. I don't know when, but Simon Wexler said he is sending a rep over to shadow us for two weeks to see if we have what it takes to be one of theirs."

"Do we have any idea who it could be?" Deepika asked.

"Probably Nene Mabuse," Haseena chimed in. "She's their head of development and international relations. She's the one who recruited Halcyon over in Kenya, their last addition."

Haseena was always on top of every information and news item.

Annabelle nodded. She'd found out the same thing when she'd gone looking online the day before. She'd also checked flights from Johannesburg, where Nene worked at the Wexler-Prinsloo headquarters. The only arrival today would be at three in the afternoon. Ample time for them to smooth all their wrinkles, plus she would already have dealt with Hector by then.

"So, everyone, once she gets here, we'll have to be even more on top of our game. At least for those two weeks, we have to be perfect, you hear me? This is the opportunity of a lifetime, and we would be idiots if we let this pass us by. As far as I know, no other agency on the whole island has ever been approached by Wexler-Prinsloo. That they even deemed us worthy is the sign we are destined for greatness, as long as we don't fuck up. Got it?"

There were mumbles and nodding all around the table.

She clapped her hands to signify the end of the meeting. The team dispersed, returning to their desks. She walked back to her office and passed by Daniel's desk in the adjoining room.

He sat with his right knee bent, foot up on the chair, his trouser leg pulled up, and his hands furiously rubbing some salve on his skin. Even from where she stood on the threshold, the chemical scent of the ointment assaulted her nostrils and made her turn away.

"Pure aloe vera gel works wonders on mosquito bites, you know," she chided.

He snorted. "On you, maybe. Not everyone has the luck of being born here and ending up with thick skin."

Daniel had been born in England to Mauritian parents and had spent his first year there. His other siblings had all been born here on the island … and none of them had any of his issues with local mosquitoes.

"Poor little Brit," she joked.

He rolled his eyes at her and went back to his salve.

She turned and made her exit before the smell could assault her once more.

What would she do without her loyal second-in-command? They joked and laughed among themselves, Daniel chiding her often and never hesitating to be the voice of reason when she let herself get carried away.

But the best thing about their relationship was the solid friendship between them that cemented their partnership. Though he always called her *'patronne'*— meaning female boss in French—Daniel knew they worked best as a team; he wouldn't go behind her back, just as she wouldn't do that to him, either. She might be the boss, but they were complementary together, like yin and yang.

Once at her desk, she sat down and opened her email inbox, quickly going through the queries Daniel or Haseena had flagged for her attention. Her work was interrupted a little while later when Deepika came in to deposit a massive bouquet of local red anthuriums and milky-white arums. The card said it was from Nina for a job well done on her event. Haseena had already told her the fashion show had been a hit in the media all through Sunday and was still being talked about this morning.

The receptionist also informed her how Hector had said he'd drop in sometime later, whenever he could.

Of course, the asshat would want everything happening on his terms. Screw him. *We'll see who has the last laugh when he hears we've been picked up by Wexler-Prinsloo.* Still, she had until the end of the day to deal with this matter then smooth everything over for the arrival of Nene Mabuse.

She pulled her cell phone and scrolled through the contacts for Nina's number. Once she had the diva on the line, she thanked her for the flowers and for having done business with their agency.

Nina gave a rollicking laugh that had her moving the phone a few inches from her ear.

"Oh, darling, I had my doubts when Hector suggested your name, but you, my girl, put all those to rest. Tell me, you don't do events on the African continent, too, do you?"

"Unfortunately, no." At least, not for the time being—they hadn't expanded beyond Mauritian territory yet, needing a robust network of contacts abroad first. If they landed the partnership …

"Shame. My next show will be in Lagos in three months. I really wish you could handle this for me. I mean, the way you managed to avert the showstopper crisis … Well, hats off to you. I'll see you sometime, then. Tootles."

Annabelle blinked as the beep of the cut call resounded in her ear. Well, it had gone well. She now had Nina Harelson as a satisfied client and could probably count on her to give Sparkle positive word of mouth out there.

And speaking of the crisis in question, whatever happened to her saviour?

She gulped as she thought, once again, of the Mystery Man who had saved her hide on Saturday night.

His sultry gaze remained at the forefront of her mind whenever she closed her eyes. The man had been sex on a stick, and sadly, it looked like it would be one of those encounters taking place once in a lifetime under seemingly magical conditions. She had no clue who he was or where to find him. Good luck combing a whole continent looking for him; not counting the thousands of East African expats all around the globe.

A sigh escaped her. She'd have to hang on to the memory of him and be satisfied.

She immersed herself back into her work.

Avignon, a world-renowned French bread and pastry shop chain which had started in the eponymous French town, was implanting itself in Mauritius. Sparkle had won the contract for the launch—event, media, the whole hoopla. The big reveal of their first shop in an exclusive little mall in the town of Curepipe further inland would be in ten days. She had her work cut out.

"Patronne!"

She looked up at an excited Daniel standing on the threshold of her office. "Hmm?"

"You are not gonna believe this!"

"Believe what?"

He came in, tugged her from her chair, and then pushed her to the side window opening onto the wrap-around porch that ran all around the dwelling. From there, she had an unencumbered view of the entrance lobby ... and what she saw had her jaw dropping open.

There, in the little vestibule with the open door, stood Mystery Man from the other night. Today, he'd dressed in a cream-coloured suit that made him look lean and lethal, but just as dangerous as in the champagne Hugo Boss attire. And she'd bet her life this one was Armani or some other Italian designer's duds.

"What is he doing here?" she hissed towards Daniel as she hurried away from the window and flattened her back to the wood wainscoting on the wall.

Daniel shrugged. "How do I know? I am *not* playing wingman to you after the last time at the bar when—"

"Okay, fine. I get it. You don't have to!" He always brought that incident up—she'd chatted up a guy who had flirted back, until his boyfriend had made his presence known and turned on Daniel, who he thought had been hitting on his man.

The intercom buzzed then. "Annabelle, someone here to see you."

So he had found her, after all. His parting promise hadn't been in vain.

She took a deep breath and psyched herself to go out to meet him. As she peeled herself from the wall, she turned to Daniel. "How do I look?"

"You actually look like a hazelnut wafer biscuit."

Right, she had worn the cream and light brown pinstripe jumpsuit today. She rolled her eyes at his help, which was anything but, and on another deep breath, she fluffed her hair and started in the direction of the lobby.

As soon as the room came into view, her step faltered. Because seeing the man across a window and seeing him up close and in person was something altogether different.

Something she wasn't ready for. The tingling in her legs returned, as did the roiling of apprehension and warning inside her stomach. Could the guy be bad news? Because she sure knew how to choose them, didn't she? The last man she had trusted had left her out of the blue one December morning and had literally fallen off the map afterwards.

Don't think of Dax.

She was so over him ... wasn't she?

She steeled her spine and marched on towards the lobby. And that's when he turned from where he'd been admiring a colourful painting by Mauritian artist Vaco Baissac on the wall with his back to her. His dark, intense gaze landed on her and almost froze her to the spot. Drat. How could his eyes seem more penetrating now? Could it be daylight versus artificial light the other night?

He broke the ice by smiling at her and starting in her direction.

"Hey," he said.

"Hey yourself," she replied as she stopped a few feet from him.

"That rain check. I'm collecting today. Told you I'd find you sometime."

She nodded, unable to say anything. His voice seemed to have this effect on her, paralyzing her, especially her vocal cords, in the most delicious manner.

"You are Annabelle de Castelban."

A statement, to which she nodded again like one of those bobble-head dogs on car dashboards.

"Zachariah Hashemi," he said and put out his hand. "Everyone calls me Zach."

She took it, and heat once again flowed into her, along with a little zing of current. Wait, her hands couldn't have gone static, right? It must be something about him, about this contact between them.

"I'm sorry I didn't introduce myself properly the other night. I should have. Simon told me to, but I wanted to meet you on neutral ground, so to speak …"

That name … The sound of his voice filtered out and seemed to be growing farther and farther away.

"Simon?" she croaked.

He furrowed his brows. "Simon Wexler. He told me he spoke with you on Friday, told you to expect someone from the agency this week."

"But, I thought …" The words died on her lips as the realization settled in. "You are the Wexler-Prinsloo rep?"

****

"I am."

Zach hid his reaction when she suddenly dropped his hand like it was a hot potato.

Was it disappointment shooting up his arm? He shook the disturbing feeling away.

"And you were assessing us that night?"

One didn't need to have trained as a spy to hear the incredulity—and the horror!—in her tone. The emotions didn't sound fake, and a part of him took a step back to really take her in.

She had dressed in a sleeveless jumpsuit that made her look like a sexy vixen on one of those retro posters. Her thick dark hair haloed her small face and fell around her shoulders in soft waves a man would love to mess up and spread all over the pillow when he had her in bed.

Bad line of thought. He caught himself as his mind started to conjure the picture with startling clarity and a level of detail that should've had him worried. He'd seen her for all of a few hours—yes, he'd watched her throughout the evening on Saturday—and he shouldn't be able to conjure up the shape of her body and the slope of her curves with such exquisite precision.

"I wasn't on the clock back then," he told her with a smile, hoping to put her at ease again.

She blinked. "And you are now, right? For the next two weeks."

He chuckled. "Like white on rice."

Aside from some more rapid blinking, she didn't let any emotion betray her. He'd give her credit. If he were in her position, knowing someone who could make or break his career was shadowing him and looking for every instance where he'd fail, he would've been cowering in his shoes.

And if she were a psychopath—if she were Evangeline—she would hide her game entirely. The rapid blinks making him think of a doll wouldn't even register. No, someone like Evangeline would lack general empathy to also feel any emotion.

But he wasn't sure of this. Not yet. So he better stay on alert.

"Fine," she said with a smile that looked a little forced. "I'll have the staff arrange an office for you."

"Don't put me in the cleaning pantry," he joked.

She had turned on her heel to lead the way inside, and she angled her body back towards him. "Now, why would I do that?"

He shrugged. "Well, having me out of the way and all. It has been known to happen to some reps."

She snorted. "Well, far from me to try and hide anything from you. Actually, do you have thick skin?"

His turn to blink. "I beg your pardon?"

She waved a hand in the air. "Mosquitoes. Do they love your blood?"

"Not that I have noticed."

"Trust me, you would have if they liked you. Come on. I have the perfect spot for you."

She led the way inside the period dwelling. He had been surprised to find this was the agency's seat. The Corpus liaison he'd been assigned on the island, an agent by the name of Jonathan Jones, had scoped the place and sent him pictures of the colonial house before he'd come in today. The building was entirely in wood, with a shingled, gabled roof, a big garden with massive mango trees in front, and a wrap-around porch on all four sides. Tall French windows opened onto said porch all over the place.

She emerged into a glassed-in conservatory with an enormous steel and glass table in the middle and a profusion of luxuriant green ferns all around in pots and hanging baskets. Some of the sofas were in white-painted wicker, and the chairs were a mix and match of metal and upholstered wood. It reminded him of something one would imagine in a setting like tropical India or Havana in Cuba.

"Here," she said. "Welcome to your office."

He nodded. "Perfect."

"You can use your laptop; plugs are down there all along the floor. Wi-Fi, of course, throughout the interior and in some parts of the garden, too. Deeps will give you the password."

"Deeps?"

"Deepika, our receptionist. Speaking of, let me introduce you to everyone."

She went back into the main hallway and bisected to the entrance lobby, where she officially introduced him to the dark-skinned, black-haired girl with too much eyeliner. Then there was Daniel, her assistant. He'd already seen the Asian guy the other night. Haseena was a fair-skinned Muslim woman with a turban hijab hiding her hair. There was Micah, a young Black man who was their courier and jack-of-all-trades the rest of the time. The other three girls were Dina, Rebecca, and Kajal. They looked like a mix of Indian and Black to him.

So Annabelle was the only White person in the whole outfit. He'd heard French-Mauritians could get very cagey, and though they worked well with the other races on the island, they kept the upper echelons of their company hierarchies filled in with people from their own world. Seemed it wasn't the case here. Should he commend her for that? A psychopath wouldn't be a proponent of equal opportunities, would they?

Annabelle let out an audible groan as she rounded the corner towards her office. Across the adjoining room, Daniel gave her a soft shrug and composed himself when he noticed Zach was watching the encounter.

A quick glance inside the other room showed him a tall White man who had, however, let himself go enjoying the good life too much. Hector Valriche did not have the frame to carry those extra pounds and the sagging jowls on his face.

Annabelle tilted her head back and seemed to be mouthing something. He narrowed his gaze on her lips—she was counting backwards from ten to one.

The clenched hands were also unfurling as she went along with the numbers. When she was done, she turned to him.

"Okay, White-on-rice. I was about to go into a partnership with this guy over there until he showed me we don't share the same values. He's getting the sack."

Zach raised his eyebrows. "He doesn't know it's coming?"

She gave a derisive soft laugh. "He wouldn't think of it even in his worst nightmare. He thinks he owns me."

Something in her tone made him turn his head sharply towards the other man. It was true that men like him in positions of power thought women to be weak and exploitable. No arsehole had the right to even think of treating a woman that way, though, and if Zach had a say, the bastard would learn this the hard way—which would involve something like waterboarding or a similar tactic.

But this was her battle to wage. He wouldn't deny her the privilege.

She took two steps towards the office, then turned to him. "You coming?"

"You want me in there?"

She rolled her eyes. "Well, if you're gonna be white-on-rice, you'll have to be privy to everything going on in here. I'm giving you the rice here."

He smiled. She had a funny way with words, this woman. He waved his hand towards the door, indicating she should go first and he'd follow her.

"Annabelle. Kept me waiting, didn't you?"

Valriche didn't even have the courtesy of getting up when she walked into the office. To her credit, she went to the other side of the desk and settled in her executive chair. Zach sat down on a settee to the side. Valriche seemed to pick up that someone else was in the room, and he turned and gave Zach the once-over, before chuckling.

"Slumming it with the male model, I see."

He restrained himself from getting up to punch that arrogant jerk in the face. Annabelle threw him a look, then she turned to Valriche.

"Something like that," she said. "None of your concern."

He wouldn't hold the apparent dismissal against her. It was part of a bigger strategy.

"So," Valriche said as he parked himself deeper into the chair and crossed one ankle over the other knee. "I'm sorry to say, my dear, the fashion show was a total flop. You really didn't handle it well, did you?"

Zach waited to see how Annabelle would react. Watching this kind of encounter would allow him to garner an accurate measure of this woman, if she were innocent or a killer in sheep's clothing.

"Really?" she asked as she mirrored Valriche's pose, minus the ankle over knee. Her ankles were crossed in a delicate duchess slant, giving her entire body poise and distinction. "That's not what I heard. In fact, Nina was just telling me this morning how it was a shame I couldn't come with her to arrange her next event in Lagos."

Valriche gulped upon hearing this. Good. The prat needed to be brought down a peg or two.

"That's not what she told me."

Annabelle just quirked an eyebrow. "This can't keep going on, Hector."

"What can't?"

"This ... partnership." She shook her head, displacing quite a few strands of hair in the process, the long locks swishing against the silk of her jumpsuit. "Not gonna work."

Valriche gave a bark of humourless laughter. "You can't get rid of me, Annabelle."

"Oh, I can. Ours was a verbal agreement only, Hector. Nothing has been signed yet."

"So this is how you're going to play it, huh? By being the head bitch in the building."

That's it. Now he really itched to send the loser's teeth flying.

"Thanks for the compliment," Annabelle said with a small smile.

"So you get me to introduce you to Nina, you get chummy with her, and then you ditch me like an old sock? Classy."

Annabelle shook her head softly. The swish of hair against silk almost hypnotized him this time, and he forced his mind off the sound to focus on the altercation taking place. He really wanted to see if she was made of sterner stuff.

"You ditched *yourself* like an old sock, Hector. I told you, after you pulled your little prank with the caterer, that I wouldn't stand for such asshattery again. Your niece almost gave everyone food poisoning by cutting corners on the ingredients in her food and pocketing the money on the side."

He sat up straighter on his seat. "Do not bring Alice into this!"

Annabelle rolled her eyes. "*You* brought her in here, not me! I told you nepotism did not work in my agency."

Valriche waved a theatrical hand in the air. "Here you go on your high horse again—"

"Cut it out. You know you fucked up. It's over, Hector."

He snapped his fingers. "Just like that? You'll ditch me just like that."

Annabelle had the good sense not to be goaded by his comment.

"Fine, Little Miss Exemplary. How do you think everyone will look at you when they hear you simply used me to land Nina's event? Everyone will know what a little sycophant you are."

Zach had expected her to blow her top off upon hearing the barely veiled threat inside Valriche's words. He was surprised when she smiled, uncrossed her arms in front of her chest, and placed her forearms on the table before leaning slightly forward.

"Bring it," she said softly.

Here was the thing—you couldn't manipulate someone confident in the knowledge that they were on the right side. She had this going for her. Her honesty rang clearly in her stance.

She couldn't be a stone-cold killer, could she?

Valriche jumped to his feet. "This isn't over."

Annabelle settled back into her seat. "It is. Goodbye, Hector. Please close the door on your way out."

She then turned her attention to a sheaf of papers on her desk, dismissing the other man royally.

Valriche muttered a few curses, and Zach almost stood after witnessing the look full of rage and hate he directed onto Annabelle before he turned on his heel and stormed out of the office, slamming the door behind him.

Annabelle seemed to wait a few moments to do anything else. When they heard the sound of a car starting and tearing out of the driveway in a screaming screech of rock chippings, she let her shoulders sag and closed her eyes.

Yes, she was made of stern stuff, but she was also human. This seemed way too genuine to be a part being played for his benefit.

But either way, he would be around her for the next two weeks. If this were an act, she was bound to slip up at some point.

He got to his feet, and the movement seemed to make her recall he was still in the room. She turned weary eyes on him, and he gave her a small smile.

"Is it like that every day?" he joked.

She seemed stunned for a second, then she laughed.

He liked the sound of her laughter. As well as the sound of her hair swishing against her clothes. It made him wonder if the locks would make the same soft swoosh when unravelled across his pillow—

Getting ahead of himself. He wasn't here for a shag. He was here to ascertain if she was a killer, and if she were, he would have to get rid of her ...

"You should go grab your stuff and get settled on the veranda," she told him.

Good idea. He nodded.

Still, on the threshold, he paused and turned to face her as something registered in his mind.

"White-on-rice, huh?"

She raised her eyebrows in question.

"I still think I prefer 'tall drink of water'," he said with a laugh.

Zach winked at her, laughing softly inside himself at the sight of the pink flush now bathing her highlighted cheekbones.

He exited the house and went to his car to get his things, his steps remarkably light considering his mission in this country.

Not for here and now, he reminded himself. He had two weeks, after all.

CHAPTER THREE

Port-Louis, Mauritius. St Georges Street
Thursday, February 5. 12.34 p.m.

Zach couldn't miss the effervescence bubbling around the office when he returned from lunch. The staff usually had food catered to them from a few delivery spots around the capital city, but he preferred to stay safe and get his own food. Until he knew for sure Annabelle wasn't the assassin his agency was after, he would be taking his precautions.

Still, the level of activity today struck him as off, and he made a beeline for her office to catch the drift of what could be happening.

"What's going on here?" he asked as he stepped over the threshold.

She stood near the tall bookshelf, pulled a few books out, and slipped them into her tote.

"Field trip," she said with a smile.

"Where to?"

She looked up and winked at him. "It's a surprise."

He hated surprises. For once, he didn't hide his emotions, and the furrow of his brow must've been evident to her.

She laughed and brushed past him, slipping the massive handbag over her shoulder. "Come on, White-on-rice. Don't tell me you're chicken."

In doing so, her free shoulder brushed the sleeve of his jacket.

The sizzle of need and longing she brought up inside him at the touch told him to clasp the well-defined, naked upper arm and propel her against the wall, his thigh between her legs, his breath fanning her lips as he showed her how much he wasn't a chicken.

But that wasn't what she'd meant, and he had no right getting involved with her, especially sexually. She was his mark, full stop.

"We'll take my car," she said from a few paces down the hallway.

He followed behind her and pulled his cell phone out, sending a quick message to Jonathan to tell him to track his location as they were leaving the premises.

True, the whole office seemed to be going—everyone was getting into cars in the courtyard, except for Deepika who remained seated at the front desk. The others were also doing a human chain, transferring nondescript cardboard boxes closed with Sellotape from the office building into the boots of every vehicle around. Still, better to be safe than sorry. He could have backup coming to help if she were leading him into an ambush.

Annabelle settled into the driver's seat of a praline-coloured Kia Picanto. The car was a few years old, if he were reading the license plate right—Mauritian cars displayed the year the vehicle had come out of the dealership brand new as the last two numbers on the registration ID. Strange, because he'd expected someone like her to drive something flashy and European, like a Mercedes or Audi SUV. Her file said she used to burn the Mauritian asphalt in a Ferrari 458 Italia.

He slid into the passenger seat, which proved tricky given his size, and he had to push the chair back as much as it would go to have enough leg room. Could they still swap for his Jaguar F-Pace rental? No, he had no clue where they were going, and GPS on this small island was surprisingly finicky, as he'd found out by uncovering some unaccounted-for shortcuts in the maze of streets around the Sparkle office in the centre of the capital.

"So, where we going to?" he asked.

"It's a surprise," she said again, with an eye roll this time.

As soon as she switched the car on, the radio started blaring, a music channel playing the latest pop songs, it seemed. Damn, he hated pop music. Annabelle slid on a pair of gigantic sunglasses that almost ate up her face, and then, they were on the road. She navigated the little streets with swift turns of the wheel, and when she wasn't softly singing along to the songs, she would loudly berate other drivers who cut in front of her or stopped abruptly or were going too slow.

Guess the consummate professional she was in the office couldn't stop herself from experiencing road rage. Though he couldn't fault her. Mauritian drivers really were dangerous, especially in Port-Louis. Soon, they reached the motorway, and she often threw quick glances at the speedometer and did not let the car go over a-hundred-and-ten kilometres an hour, the speed limit on those dual carriageways.

Out here, he recognized the landmarks and the roads—he took this same route every day to his hotel in Balaclava, a small coastal village to the north of Port-Louis and where Annabelle had her residence. The Corpus had put him in a nearby hotel so he could keep tabs on her outside the office.

However, they turned at a roundabout well before the exit leading to her home. This area looked a bit derelict, concrete buildings giving way to automobile shops, then a sort of low-quality housing zone that reminded him of poverty-ridden pockets all over Central Africa. Lots of Black kids were playing ball on the streets, and they would move out of the way when they saw the car coming.

He was stunned when Annabelle waved at them, and they waved back with smiles and loud hollers. Looked like they knew her around here.

The car continued on its ride until they drew close to the seaside—he could see a signboard indicating the public beach three hundred metres away after a turn to the left. *Baie du Tombeau*, the region was called. Bay of the tomb. Macabre or what?

They went farther along the main road, and Annabelle stopped the car at a vast, wrought-iron gate. She lowered her window and pressed the intercom button. When the gate slid open, she sped them through a driveway and stopped the vehicle in the parking area of the courtyard. The other cars from the agency followed suit, then everyone alighted to go get the cardboard boxes from the boots. Strangely, Annabelle didn't unload anything from her car.

"Hey, White-on-rice," she called out as she pushed her sunglasses on top of her head. "Make yourself useful."

She came up to him and dumped a big box in his hands. He almost lost his breath because the thing was heavy. She didn't seem to have broken sweat, though. Now he had a fair idea where those muscles on her upper arms must come from.

"What do I do with this?" he asked.

"Follow me."

He started after her. Out of the corner of his eye, he saw quite a few curtains twitching at the many windows on one side of the low, single-level building.

The ramp next to the steps leading to the porch further tickled his curiosity, and he got his answer when he looked up and spotted the name of the establishment: *Bon Espoir Retirement and Care Facility*.

They were at an old people's home.

What were they doing here?

He sidled closer to Annabelle and asked her the question. She didn't have time to reply because a portly woman in a white doctor's coat flew down on her and grabbed her shoulders to kiss her on both cheeks. The women started an animated conversation in French, which he had no trouble following—one of the two official languages in Djibouti was French.

But he had purposely led Annabelle to believe that he had no grasp over it so she might let her guard down around him in situations where French or Creole was warranted.

He figured out from the talks that the doctor was happy about their visit, telling Annabelle how much the residents had been waiting for her to return and see them.

So this was a regular thing. Good to know.

The doctor then directed the other Sparkle staff members towards a room at the back, where they all went with their boxes. When the woman made to take the one in his hands, he didn't know if he should relinquish it or be the gentleman and carry it for her to the far room. But her grip proved deceptively strong; she had dislodged the cardboard from his hands and carried it away before he could blink.

When he turned towards Annabelle to ask her what the hell was going on, his senses went onto high alert, the tingling at the back of his neck imparting that danger lurked in the surroundings. Could it be Evangeline? One of her associates?

But then, he noticed the pack of three old women with white hair like wispy candy floss converging onto Annabelle. She squealed when she saw them and bent almost in two to hug each of the diminutive creatures. A babble of French words started, and she laughed as she reached into her tote. Pulling out the books he'd seen her remove from the bookshelf at the office, she gave them to the women.

"Oh, it's the next in the series by Sabrina Jeffries. And a Jojo Moyes book, too. Dan Brown! You always bring the best stuff. Now, about sneaking in some gin …"

The gaggle of golden girls prattled on, then one of them elbowed Annabelle in the ribs and lowered her voice. He could still hear her, though.

"Who is this delicious morsel with you?" she asked.

The others joined the fray. "He looks like that hot surgeon on *Code Black* who is always angry. Though the man is perfectly in his rights, his wife abandoned him and their sick baby, after all."

"Is he your new boyfriend, Annabelle? Yes, he is! He must be! Look how you're blushing!"

Indeed, she *was* blushing, Zach found once he'd gotten past the disagreeable sensation of feeling like a piece of meat being carefully considered in a market place.

Annabelle laughed. "No, he isn't. He is a business partner from abroad."

One of the women huffed. "Ha. Bed partner is what I'd make him if I had twenty years less. Don't tell me it hasn't crossed your mind, *ma fille.*"

She laughed some more, though it sounded a little forced to him. Wrapping her arms around the shoulders of two of the women, she hugged them to her. "Come on, you naughty bitches. Off you go for tea."

She gently propelled all three of them towards the far room, then she turned around and faced him.

"Thank God for small favours," she mumbled.

"I beg your pardon?"

"Nothing. You don't understand French, right?"

He shook his head.

The sigh of relief she gave literally deflated her and made her shoulders sag. "Thank God."

"So," he started, waving his hands around to encompass the place which was, now that he looked at it more closely, a recreational lobby. Comfortable, thickly upholstered sofas and some high-backed chairs surrounded him, and a wide flat screen TV hung on one wall. "What's all this?"

She smiled as she threw a wistful look around. "Corporate social responsibility."

He blinked. "What?"

She rolled her eyes at him. "We don't just cut a cheque to this place every quarter and turn our backs on them. Part of what we do at Sparkle is engage ourselves in the social aspects of what our CSR endeavours cover."

"And you're doing this here today how?" He threw his hands up at the way her eyes narrowed dangerously on him. "Not being an arse. Just asking to try and make sense."

"Look at this place, Zach. These are old people who might or might not have families out there, but for all intents and purposes, their being here means everyone else has washed their hands of them. Do you know what old people suffer most from? Loneliness. So once every two months, we come down here and bring them cakes and other such goodies. We have tea with them when it is served here at two o'clock and spend some time talking with them."

Something inside his chest grew tight and started hurting. In his mind, he found himself shrinking to barely four feet high, his hand in his mother's gentle grip. In her other hand, she held the fingers of his little sister. He remembered how she released them and got down on her haunches to look into their faces, smiling, before telling them something about doing good and being good. Funnily enough, she, too, had brought them to an old people's home that day, and her words had sounded a lot like what Annabelle had just told him.

The room seemed to close in around him, and he suddenly found it hard to breathe. He should get out of here. Memories of his past, especially of his late mother, did not sit well with him. Generally, he did everything to forget about it.

He blinked as a worried Daniel approached, and he shook himself out of his spell so he could grasp what was going on. Something was wrong; he could feel it.

The young man drew close to Annabelle and spoke to her in low tones that however weren't hushed enough to cut him out and make them sound rude by alienating him.

"Deeps just called," Daniel said in a rushed spiel. "Says Margot Dupuis rang to say she would be running late and if you could move her appointment to two-thirty."

Annabelle gaped at him. "Margot Dupuis? What is she talking about?"

Daniel's jaw clenched, and his tone lowered further. "You forgot to input it in the calendar."

"I did not!" she hissed back.

"Annabelle, this is the second time this week—"

"Margot must have it wrong."

"You seriously think she would just conjure up an appointment and dump it on us?"

"I ..." She shook her head. "*Merde!*"

"It's almost two. If you leave now, you can make it back before she swans in."

She threw a look at the thin rose gold watch on her wrist. "You're right. Tell everyone I'm sorry I had to bail. I will make it up to them next time."

"Go," Daniel told her.

Annabelle started towards the door, then her gaze landed on Zach, and she paused. "You can catch a ride back with the others?"

Daniel chimed in. "We came in two cars, *patronne*. We're already jam-packed."

"It's okay," Zach replied. "I'll come back with you."

He had no intention or desire to be here. Not when he'd just thought of his mother who he had lost at the tender age of six. Thirty years ago, and the mere thought of her still hit him like a sucker punch to the gut. She had been the epitome of everything good in this world, unlike the despicable witch his father had married after her death because he'd needed to give his children a mother again. The old man had never realized how no one could ever replace the woman who had given birth to him and his sister.

A touch of crimson painted itself on Annabelle's pale cheeks, and without a word, she stalked out and to her car, closing the door with way too much force. He followed and got in, also.

Once she'd started on the road, he took a deep breath. "What happened?"

He would play the ignorant fool and make as if he hadn't understood their rushed talk in Creole. They had reverted to English when talking to him. Would Annabelle fib and worm her way out of this, or would she own up to her shit?

She remained silent for a long moment, then she sighed, not taking her gaze off the road in front of her. "Meeting with a client at the office. I made a mistake … forgot I had scheduled it for today."

He was floored for the better part of a minute. So she had actually come clean and told him the truth?

"That doesn't shine a good light on you," he said.

He was surprised when she drew the car to a stop. Ahead of them, the little kids were still playing with an old football on the dirty, dusty street.

"If you think so," she finally quipped. Then, she turned to face him. "You'll come to find, Zach Hashemi, that with me, it is very much take it or leave it."

On those cutting words, she exited the car, opened the boot, and walked towards the kids with a big cardboard box balanced in her hands. The children swarmed around her, and she went with them to where a few older Black men sat at a rickety table playing dominoes under the sprawling branches of a banyan tree. They cleared the surface for her, and she deposited the box. The kids all plunged in to retrieve some pastry and a carton of juice.

Zach got out of the car and propped his thigh against the hood, crossing his arms in front of him as he watched her being the social butterfly with these people who obviously looked like they came from a socially disadvantaged neighbourhood.

One of the old men tipped his hat in Zach's direction.

"To ti copain sa?" he asked.

Annabelle laughed. "Non, do. Ene collegue, sa, sa em tou."

Is he your boyfriend, the old man had asked. He'd had no trouble understanding, Creole being so similar to French. To which she'd replied that Zach was nothing but a colleague.

The squeezing in his chest returned, but this time, with a different emotion. Because the crazy thing was, he suddenly wanted to be more than 'just a colleague' for her. It had been funny when the old women had ribbed her, but they had been White, like her. Watching her with these folks here, the people with the simple life, he saw who she was really, deep inside of her.

A woman with a heart of gold.

She couldn't be a cold assassin who got her kicks out of killing her marks in the most twisted ways imaginable.

He refused to believe it, but as long as he didn't have proof of this, nothing could come of their association. As long as he hadn't proven who Evangeline really was, his hands would be tied.

And herein lay the real question—who was Evangeline really? Had they been barking up the wrong tree here, focusing on Annabelle de Castelban as their target?

Something like deep conviction pooled in his gut to settle like rapidly solidifying cement. They had to widen the search for Evangeline. Pulling his phone out, he sent Jonathan a quick text telling him they had better go through all their intel again later today.

When he next looked up, it was to find Annabelle had started in his direction. However, the children had hijacked her into playing ball with them, and he watched with raised eyebrows as she expertly dribbled the football around their nimble legs and scored a goal into the post, which was simply two pieces of rock placed five feet apart on the old asphalt road.

He glanced at her feet—she had worn trainers today. A far cry from her usual stiletto heels.

She had known she would be coming here to play ball with those kids.

Awe filled him. Would she never stop surprising him?

As she got into the car, he settled back in and tugged his seat belt on. She started them on the road to Port-Louis again, the radio blaring once more as she'd reached over to turn the volume up. Guess it meant he was dismissed.

She didn't say a word all the way to the office, and less than a minute after they'd gotten into the colonial house, a car entered the courtyard, and the client came out. Annabelle swanned out of the lobby and opened her arms wide to embrace the boho-chic White woman outside.

As she passed by him in the hallway, she cocked an eyebrow. "You coming?"

He shook his head. "Not this time."

Both eyebrows went up at this, but she didn't add a word and followed the other woman into her office.

Zach went by the veranda and grabbed his laptop from the table, then made his way to his Jag. Jonathan would be waiting for him at the hotel. They had work to do.

He should forget about Annabelle de Castelban for a few hours and look at all their intel with a new, more objective eye.

***

Port-Louis, Mauritius. St Georges Street
Friday, February 6. 10.25 a.m.

Annabelle looked up from her computer screen when her senses told her someone stood at the door. No, not someone. Zach.

The tingling returned in her hands, and she had to peel her fingers from where they had been flying over the keyboard to keep from typing in lines of gibberish.

He had worn a dark, slate-grey suit today. So far, she had only seen him in light colours. The contrast with his amber skin had been startling in those cases, but against the dark backdrop, he positively smouldered. The sharp lines made him look even leaner and rugged like he had ruthless energy being contained inside the well-defined tailored set. The dark tones should've made him look smaller, not larger than life as usual, but strangely, they did the opposite, defining his broad shoulders with much more cut precision.

A little breath puffed out of her at the sight, and she blinked to make her thoughts return to a semblance of a regular pattern.

He took one step into the office and gestured with a broad sweep of his hands. "Where is everyone?"

She frowned at him. He didn't know?

"It's a public holiday. Chinese New Year."

His eyebrows rose. "I thought Sunday had been a public holiday already."

"It was. February One commemorates the abolition of slavery."

"How many of these do you have in a year?"

"Public holidays? Fifteen."

Surprise registered on his face. A lot of people had the same reaction when they heard that.

"One for the major festival of every religion, bar for Jewish people as there's only a handful of them on the island," she explained. "Plus there's the regular stuff like New Year, Christmas, Independence Day, the abolition of slavery, the arrival of Indian indentured labourers, Labour Day. Catholics get a toss-up every year as it's either the Feast of the Virgin Mary in August or All Saints' Day in November—"

"Wait. You can remember all this?"

She shrugged.

"Every Mauritian remembers all this, duh." She nodded at him. "So, you woke up this morning and didn't realize something was amiss? Like less traffic on the roads, all the shops closed?"

He frowned. "There *was* less traffic."

"There you go."

The sound of firecrackers resounded outside, and he flinched.

"Ah, the *Tongshu* must've said how ten-thirty was the most appropriate time to set off the firecrackers so the light and sounds would repel the *Nianshou.*"

"What?"

"I hope you closed the front door on the way in." She had to shout over the many bursts of firecrackers starting off all around them. "We're gonna choke on all the smoke."

She got out of her chair and took a turn into the hallway to find he had indeed closed the front door.

"Great tactic to asphyxiate the *Nian* monster, Daniel's father maintains, but I reserve judgement on that," she said as she brushed past him back into the room. "It's okay, baby," she cooed, going to the tabby cat that had gotten up from where he'd been perching on top of the bookshelf.

Zach stepped farther into the room and eyed the cat with a baleful eye. Movement came from the other side, near the French windows, and his gaze cut to the big pet bed with two other felines lounging on it.

"You brought your cats to the office?"

"Of course I did. I couldn't leave them at home where they might get scared of the sound of the firecrackers. As long as they can see me, they won't drum up a fuss. Plus with Daniel not here for the foreseeable future, they can stay without any risk of the citronella candle fumes affecting them."

"Daniel is on leave?"

She nodded. "Takes a few days off after the Chinese New Year every year. I can promise you're not gonna find any Chinese person in any office until at least next Tuesday."

"So you're holding the fort on your own?" he asked as he seemed to gather his wits and went to the sofa where he sat down.

She released the tabby back onto the bookshelf and went by the cat bed to pet the other two on the head—it wouldn't pay to have any of them jealous.

"Everyone will rally around come tomorrow. That's how it is here."

"It's very generous."

She shrugged. "Well, everyone gets something out of it. In a few weeks, Deepika, Kajal, and Dina will be going on the Hindu pilgrimage to the sacred crater lake of Grand Bassin. They'll get a few days off that week. During Ramadan, Haseena leaves the office at three so she can go home to prepare the meal to break the fast every evening. Micah will take a day or two off for Easter, the feast of the Assumption if it isn't a public holiday that year, and the pilgrimage to the vault of the blessed *Père Laval* in September. See, everyone wins."

He shook his head. "How do you know all this?"

She laughed at this. "How can I *not* know? All this is taught in the curriculum of second or third grade in primary school."

"And all those things you were saying about the smoke and the Nan?"

"The *Nian*," she corrected. "Legend says it is a half-lion, half-bull monster who comes into houses at night to eat people and animals. It doesn't like the colour red, bright lights, and sharp noises."

"Hence, the red firecrackers."

She settled down behind her desk. "Exactly. And the *Tongshu* is a sort of almanac Chinese people use to figure out the most auspicious time for just about everything. A bit like the *Kundli* Hindu people get from Vedic astrologers that gives them their chart based on their exact time and location of birth."

"Learned all this at school?"

"Mostly from mixing and mingling with people. Mauritius is, after all, a melting pot of cultures and religions."

"That's very true." He settled back on the sofa. "You've always lived here?"

"It's home."

"As simple as that, eh? Your family has been here long, I suppose."

"Since the eighteenth century. Though my strain comes from the late nineteenth century."

He blinked. "Excuse me, what?"

She waved a hand in the air. "My great-great-grandfather. He wasn't originally from the branch of the family to settle here during French reign. When the heir and the spare died without male progeniture in the plague of 1899, he inherited it all and reluctantly came to live here. He was the black sheep, you see, a soldier in French Indo-China at the time. Brought his Indo-Chinese wife with him. The good society here did not like it, as you can imagine."

"Indo-China, eh?"

She nodded. "Yes, that's why I have eyes that look Asian."

His eyes grew wide. "I didn't say anything!"

"Didn't have to. I get the question a lot."

"Are you always so forthcoming about everything?"

"My life is an open book." She shrugged. "What about you?"

They didn't know much about him, actually. Would he open up to her?

"I was born in Tanzania."

He didn't add anything else, and she didn't pry. If he'd wanted her to know more, he wouldn't have stopped talking.

"So, who are these?" he asked, gesturing towards the cats.

She could recognize a deflection when she saw one. Fine.

"Riri, Fifi, and Loulou. The ginger butterball in the bed is Riri. The little white one next to him is Fifi. The tabby up there is Loulou."

He chuckled. "Funny names."

"Huey, Dewey, and Louie. Know those?"

He frowned. "Donald Duck's nephews, if I'm not mistaken."

"Yup. Their names in the French versions are Riri, Fifi, and Loulou."

Zach laughed. "Fitting. So, what are you working on?"

Right, work. They weren't here to have fun.

"Margot Dupuis' project," she replied.

"The client you met yesterday."

She nodded. And speaking of yesterday …

"Zach, I need to apologize for the rude way I spoke to you in the car on the way back."

He lifted an eyebrow. Guess he'd worm it out of her, then. So be it.

"I'm sorry. Those words were unwarranted."

He remained silent for long seconds, which made her squirm.

Finally, he spoke. "There was no need for excuses. You're human, like the rest of us."

He was giving her an easy out here. She couldn't take it, though. The fate of her agency might hang in this man's hands, but she had always vowed to be true to herself, and anyone who wanted to see Sparkle's every facet should see hers, too.

"I promised myself a long time ago, I would never play the victim. I've seen people do this too much around me—" She stopped talking, wondering why on Earth she was telling him this much.

"Someone in particular?"

She was saved from having to reply when her cell phone beeped with an incoming message. She raised a finger in the air, silently telling Zach to wait, then replied the text from Micah.

"If you don't mind, I don't really want to talk about that," she told him.

He remained solemn, then nodded. "So, your new project?"

She jumped on the line like a lifebuoy. "Margot Dupuis is a leading local artisanal jewellery maker. So far, she has been selling her creations through word of mouth, and once a year, she opens up the front room of her house in Calodyne in the north of the island for a private sale. But she now wants to get a sort of pop-up store venture going, where she would showcase her wares and also those of other rising Mauritian designers and artists."

"I can hear the excitement in your voice," he said.

She had to quell the smile threatening to burst on her lips.

"So why is this a great idea, and why now?"

Everyone in the communications and ads business knew how the timing was one of the most crucial components in every campaign.

She leaned forward and placed her forearms on the table. "March twelve is Independence Day. As such, March and subsequently April are months when patriotism is at its all-time high, so having pop-ups showcasing local talent at major malls and shopping centres is very good for business. They are usually booked months in advance, but someone pulled out from a mall in the North, and Margot snagged the spot, wants Sparkle to put it all together now."

"And let me guess, March twelve is another public holiday."

She grinned.

They heard the front door open, and seconds later, Micah came in with a plastic bag loaded with white Styrofoam takeout containers.

"Thanks, Micah."

"No problem." He saluted and left.

Zach turned towards the door then back at her. "He came in just to bring you food?"

"To bring *us* food. And he volunteered. He lives just a few blocks down, across the boulevard to the south, on Wellington Street."

She pulled the plastic bag towards her and started removing the containers, then placed the little pouches of chilli paste and garlic water to the side.

Suddenly, a thought chimed in. "You're not allergic to shellfish, I hope."

"No."

"Good." She frowned at him when he remained in his seat. "Well, come on up. There's some fried rice for you, as well."

He eyed the food with concentration evident on his face. What could be his problem?

Then, two and two added themselves up in her head. "It's Halal."

He blinked. "Sorry?"

"Micah orders this from a little place on Wellington Street that's operated by a Muslim woman. So the food is Halal and has no traces of pork in it." He still looked sceptical. "Well, you are a Muslim, right?"

"What made you think so?"

Had she been wrong in her assessment? All the clues pointed in that direction, though. "Well, your name, for starters. It sounds Muslim, no offence, and Tanzania has a big Muslim population, doesn't it?"

She waited with bated breath for him to answer.

"Right. On both counts."

A sigh of relief escaped her. Talk of the faux pas she'd have made if she'd gotten this wrong.

"How do you know about Halal and all that? Haseena?" he asked as he got up and came to settle in the visitor's chair across her at her desk.

"Again, just general knowledge. Everyone here knows Muslims don't eat pork and need their meat slaughtered as per Halal Islamic rites. Trust me, a restaurant persisting in not serving Halal food on the island better be very sure of its market because

Muslims are some of the biggest consumers of fast or restaurant food. It is said food courts operate at a loss during Ramadan when Muslims are fasting from dawn to dusk for thirty days."

"Really?" he said with a frown.

She nodded.

He opened the carton of egg, chicken, and shrimp fried rice, and she handed him a fork from the bag. He eyed the little packets to the side, watched her pour the garlic water sauce all over her rice and then dump on a parcel of bright green chilli paste on top.

"You gonna have that?" she asked, pointing to the chilli pack accompanying his container.

"No. What's the other sauce?"

She reached for his chilli and added it to her rice, as well. He raised his eyebrows at her.

"It's a sort of sauce made with salt, sugar, vinegar, and pounded garlic," she explained. "It accompanies all Chinese food here."

"Is it good?"

She pointed at her yet-untouched rice. "Try some, see if you like it."

"You don't mind?"

She shook her head. "Go ahead."

He reached over with his fork and picked up a bit of her rice away from the green patches of chilli. His face broke into a smile after he'd swallowed the morsel. "That's actually not bad."

"Have yours."

He snipped the corner off his garlic sauce packet and rained it all over his rice.

They ate in silence for a while.

"Good?" she asked, hissing between her teeth afterwards because of the burn of the chilli on her tongue.

He looked up at her with eyes agog.

She rolled her eyes at him. "Your food—*hiss*—is it—*hiss*—good?—*hiss*."

"You've gone all red, Annabelle. Do you always eat this much chilli?"

She nodded vigorously, hissing between words as she spoke. "It's a Mauritian thing. And hardly how much I'd eat in the restaurant."

When she'd finished, he threw his head back and laughed. The same rich sound he had bestowed upon her on the night of the fashion show. Zach Hashemi seemed to laugh like he did everything else in his life— in no half measures.

Was he the same way in bed, too?

She slapped herself inwardly at the wanton thought and propelled her body out of the chair to go to the mini-fridge in the kitchen across the hallway. She returned with two ice-cold bottles of water and handed him one. He didn't need to know how she had pressed hers to her flaming cheeks on the way back.

A sound from outside made him jerk his head up.

"Not the usual time, I know," she said. "You of all people should know the call for the *Jummah* prayer on Fridays comes earlier than every day's midday prayer."

"General knowledge again?" he asked with a little smile.

"I'm Mauritian, dude! This is the country where a few paces from one of the biggest mosques on the island is the gate marking the entrance of Chinatown."

He seemed lost in thoughts, and something niggled at her. She didn't know where she picked up the courage to ask the loaded question that came next.

"You're not religious?"

He took a deep breath. "Can't say I am, to be honest."

"Oh." She paused. "Still, I thought the Friday prayer was non-negotiable? I know quite a few Muslims who call themselves wayward but never miss this day's calling."

He lowered his head to glance at his now empty container of fried rice. His features scrunched themselves in concentration, then he got up and faced her.

"You know, I think it's not a bad idea," he said.

"What is not a bad idea?" He had lost her there.

"The *Jummah* prayer. I suppose the mosque is near, to be hearing the call of the muezzin so loudly?"

He'd been around for close to a week and didn't know there was a colossal mosque not four houses down this road from the office? He must really not be religious. But to everyone his or her beliefs—she wasn't one who would harp on being religiously correct.

"Go," she told him as he started to gather his empty food container. "They say the first row is the best spot to nab, right? Bigger blessings and all? If you go now, you'll make it before the masses."

He paused in his step. "Annabelle de Castelban, you are a woman of many surprises."

Somehow, funnily enough, these hushed words in his deep voice made her blush. Like they held so much more, so many secrets that he wasn't telling her yet.

She couldn't dwell on it, though. He was the man who would make or break Sparkle. Nothing could come from it.

"Go," she told him, shooing him away.

He stopped on the threshold. "Thank you."

She smiled—what else could she do? But inside, she started praying for when he'd finally leave. Because getting chummy and close like this to Zach would bring nothing good for her heart. The organ had been trampled on so much already—she'd be a fool to offer it on a platter for it to get destroyed again.

CHAPTER FOUR

Port-Louis, Mauritius. St Georges Street
Friday, February 6. 1.40 p.m.

Zach emerged from the mosque amid a crowd of men. Little clusters formed all over the pavement, the camaraderie and family feel in those groups evident to everyone. With today being a public holiday, the men wouldn't have to rush back to their offices, so they could loiter around for a chat.

Seeing them so chummy made his chest squeeze. He missed his family. Without him being able to think twice about the notion, his hand had reached into his jacket pocket for his phone, and he was scrolling through the contacts for a particular number.

She picked up after the third ring, her voice low and breathy.

"Hey, Zayn," he said with a smile in his voice.

"Zach! Now that's a surprise," his sister, Zenobia, replied.

"Caught you at a bad time?" he asked.

"Nah. Just finished giving vaccination shots to the kids of a village school here. Libby lost the coin toss and is thus checking all the little boys' balls to see if they are growing as they should."

He laughed in reply.

"So, how are you?" she asked. "And what made you think of me?"

"I always think of you, no matter where you are in the world."

Currently, she was posted at a hospital in the Indian coastal state of Goa, the latest place aid organization Angelos was helping out. He'd gotten his doctor sister in with them as soon as she'd finished medical school, thus able to keep an eye on her. He'd also worked for Angelos for a long time as a security consultant. Few knew it had been his cover for special ops for the Corpus—Angelos, despite being a full-fledged aid NGO, was also one of the many fronts of the clandestine agency.

"So you say," she shot back.

He heard sounds of children laughing and shrieking in the backdrop. She must've gone outside.

"You okay, Zayn?"

"I'm good. How about you? Still in Djibouti?"

"Not for the time being. I'm handling something in Mauritius right now."

"Perfect. This time, you won't send me any negative vibe because my house is a beachfront hut, what with you being on a tropical island and all."

"Hey, I never send you negative vibes!"

"Yeah, yeah, so you say."

He paused for a moment, wondering if he should tell her about what he had on his heart. But if not her, then who?

"Something made me think of Mum yesterday," he said.

She remained silent for a long time. They both missed her something fierce.

"Have you spoken to him lately?" she asked.

"No," he clipped out.

He rarely, if ever, reached out to his father. The man, who was so totally pussy-whipped by his second wife and fawning over their precious, freckle-faced son, never called him, either. No, he and Zenobia were the mixed-race offspring of their pale, green-eyed Ismaili father who could pass for a White man and the Black Somali refugee his mosque had taken in.

It had been love at first sight, their mother had always said. Zach had trouble believing his father could ever love someone. There'd been no love left for him and Zayn once their mother had suddenly passed from a brain aneurysm. Their father hadn't known what to do with them and had rushed into marrying the first gold digger who'd made googly eyes at the wealthy industrialist.

His jaw clenched, and he forced himself to release the tension and return to the phone conversation.

"So," he said. "Anyone I should come punch in the face?"

She chuckled. "If there were, I wouldn't tell you, because you would ruin his pretty face." She paused. "You know I'm not cut out for that, right?"

He did. Zenobia had borne the brunt of their wicked stepmother's wrath, because she'd ended up being the spitting image of their beautiful mother, her skin a few shades lighter, though. As such, she had a wounded heart she never wanted to open to anyone but him.

"I'm due a break after I'm done here," he told her. Alexis wouldn't begrudge him some vacation time, surely. "How about I come around and see you sometime?"

"You know what, that's an excellent idea. Will get you to loosen up a bit," she said with a laugh.

"I'm not uptight!" he chided.

"Yeah, so you say. I bet you're in a suit and tie in what must be thirty-five-degree Celsius heat right now."

"I'm not wearing a tie." Ties were too formal for Sparkle.

"Same difference."

He paused in his step when he realized he was standing in front of the wrought-iron railing of the three-storey French Embassy on St Georges Street. He'd walked well past the agency's office.

"Okay, sis, you take care of yourself, eh? I'll let you know about that trip."

"Great," she replied. "Zach? Love you," she added.

"Love you even more," he said softly, his heart threatening to burst with the feelings he had for this girl.

"Bye," she said and cut the call.

She knew he never liked saying this word.

Damn, he missed her. It had been close to a year since he'd last seen her. This trip to Goa was long overdue.

But that wasn't for the here and now. He needed to deal with the situation at hand first. And the more he thought about it, the more his gut was telling him they had the wrong mark. Annabelle couldn't be Evangeline. The assassin was a psychopath so devoid of empathy, she wouldn't even have the ability to fake an emotion, because she wouldn't know what it felt like.

Annabelle wore her heart on her sleeve. He'd seen it the day before with the old people and the street kids, then today with her cats. Plus, she really was an open book. She hid nothing, and he hadn't been able to find any secrets regarding her or even her family.

Something was amiss in this whole thing, and he'd get to the bottom of it.

A drop of water plopped on his head, and he looked up at the dense cover of grey clouds hanging low on the sky. Even the air smelled like rain, the wind picking up with the distinctive scent of water. He hurried his step and had entered the courtyard of the colonial house when the skies ripped open and let the downpour surge down. His jacket was a mess by the time he managed to duck into the lobby.

He shrugged it off, sighing in relief to find his shirt was still dry. Passing by the kitchen, he went in and draped the jacket across the back of a chair so it could air out a bit. He then made his way to Annabelle's office.

"I didn't know you got rains like this here," he said as he got in.

She looked up from her computer screen. "Oh, you don't know the half of it. Wait for it …"

"Wait for what?"

A zing of light burst outside followed seconds later by the screech of thunder.

A panicked mewl came from the pet bed.

"It's okay, Fifi." She jumped out of her chair and dropped to her knees next to the bed to pet the white cat. "*Ça va aller, m'amour. Maman est là.*"

'*It will be all right, my little love. Mummy's here.*' That's what she'd just told the little cat, and as she lifted him up from the bed, Zach's eyes grew wide.

"Wait a second. Fifi lacks one leg?"

She cuddled the little fluff ball and shushed him when another growl of thunder rumbled. "They think it was a hit and run when he was a kitten. They managed to save his life at the shelter, but had to amputate his right front leg."

Seeing this sealed something inside him. This woman just couldn't be a stone-cold killer. Especially not the kind Evangeline was.

"You took him in from the shelter?" he asked.

"Who else would? I had sworn when I started Sparkle and had to give away my cats because I was hardly at home that I would never get a pet again. They steal your heart, you know. But I made the mistake of being at the shelter that day, and the cunning vet showed me Fifi, then Riri who was an adult cat being passed on for adoption because he was no longer a kitten. Loulou never let anyone close to him, but he walked over to me and wrapped his tail around my leg. Plus them being males, it was another strike against them. Everyone wants female cats who are supposedly gentler in nature."

"You were a goner." He chuckled.

"Exactly. And they've got me wrapped around their little paws, right?" She lifted Fifi and rubbed the tip of her nose against the cat's. "I'm sorry, Zach. When there's thunder, and I'm around them, they hardly let me do anything but stay with them."

He shrugged. "It's okay. You mentioned when you started Sparkle. How did you get started, if I may ask?"

Her file said how, but he wanted to hear it from her. He was starting to reckon that he loved listening to this woman talk with the lilting lift in her soft voice.

"I worked in PR, and it got to a point where everyone was telling me I should start my own agency because I was pulling off every event and my bosses were the ones reaping the bragging rights. Clients said they'd follow me, and after a while, I believed I could do it. I didn't want to be under the thumb of a business partner or a bank, though, so to finance the whole thing, I sold the Ferrari an ex-boyfriend had given me and used the money to start Sparkle up."

So that's where the Ferrari had gone—the Corpus report had just said she had ditched it. She must have good business sense to have thought this way. Plus, she didn't have to answer to anyone, on top of it. She had, after all, said she was a 'take it or leave it' type of person.

"Your family must be very proud of you."

The more he dug, the more information he would have about her, and the more he could prove she wasn't Evangeline. Nothing would make him think she was the assassin now. Whoever had written the report on her had been biased, wanting to paint her as the famed killer.

At this, she shrugged, and a veil of darkness settled on her face.

Zach grimaced. "Sore spot? I'm sorry for asking."

She remained silent for a few moments, but then, she shook her head. "It's ... complicated. I'm an only child, and after my father died, the grass hadn't even grown on his grave when my mother was marrying his brother, my uncle."

He raised his eyebrows in surprise. That did suck.

"Very Hamlet-like, right? she continued. "Which makes me Hamleta. Which kinda sounds like ham omelette. One of my cousins teases me by those names." She cocked her head to the side. "What about you, Zach? Any family?"

The make or break moment. If she weren't his mark, after all ... what did he have to lose? Something was brewing inside him for this woman. Try as he wanted, he couldn't ignore it.

"I have a sister. We're close." Could he continue? He wanted to open up to her, though ... "Our mother died when we were small. Our father remarried soon after, but we fell to the wayside as his new wife preferred to focus on their son, and he went along with it."

Annabelle's face looked stricken. "Oh, Zach. I'm so sorry."

Strangely, he detected empathy in her tone.

"Takes one to know one?" he ventured to ask.

She nodded slowly. "Yeah. My mother also doesn't care about me since she remarried."

Who'd have thought they would find common ground this way? Still, she looked so forlorn. He didn't like seeing her this way, much preferring when she laughed and had a merry twinkle in her eye.

"So, should I start calling you Hamleta, then?"

She rolled her eyes at him. "And make me sound like a stuck-up snob from the French Revolution era? Thanks, but I have no intention of thinking of myself being guillotined."

He laughed. She sure had a sense of humour, this woman.

Outside, the sounds of the downpour started to fade. She turned to look out the window, then faced him again.

"Would you mind if we cut today short? I best get these guys back home where they'll be able to go safely cower under my bed if there's any more thunder."

The image of her bed popped in his mind—he sure wouldn't mind if she invited him to wait out the thunderstorm under her sheets.

He shook his head and forced his mind away from that picture. Nothing could happen between them. His focus now had to be on uncovering who Evangeline really was. Any day now, Alexis could call and reroute him to another country if they found any indication of the assassin's presence elsewhere.

Annabelle tried to place Fifi in the bed, but the cat whimpered in protest. Zach had hardly a second to process that she was coming his way when she pushed the cat smack against his solar plexus and his arms came up in reflex to hold the fluff ball. Fifi didn't seem at all stunned, unlike him, and bumped his little head against Zach's stomach.

Carefully, he cradled the cat with his left arm and used his right hand to pet the fluffy head. Fifi rubbed against his palm, the sounds of his purrs getting louder.

"You must be a good guy. Fifi is the best judge of character I know," Annabelle said as she stepped back into the office with a large kennel-type pet carrier in her arms.

He raised his eyes both at the carrier and at her words. Because she was right—animals were excellent judges of character. A handicapped kitten like Fifi would hardly have bonded with a psychopath devoid of empathy.

She went to the pet bed and gathered the slightly obese Riri up and placed him in the carrier. Next, she took Fifi from him, and his empty arm suddenly felt strange, like it wanted to keep holding on to the warm little ball of fur. Next, she went to the bookshelf, and Zach winced at the sound of cat claws scratching against the surface—she was having a hard time prying Loulou from the perch. The cat growled menacingly and started to howl like the undead when she managed to dislodge him and then carried him over to the carrier, where he resisted going in. She expertly manoeuvred him in, though, and had the front latch closed a minute later. Loulou's howls intensified.

"Anyone would think I was eviscerating him," she said with frustration evident in her tone.

"He's not a fan of the carrier?" Zach asked.

"Not at all. You should hear how he cries when I get him into the single cat carrier to go to the vet."

He chuckled. "You seem to have them in hand."

"Ha. I wish." She went back to her desk and settled her tote over her shoulder, then retraced her steps and crouched and picked up the carrier, standing back upright in a graceful flow.

That thing looked heavy. He should get it from her. He made a move to pick the box from her, but she laughed and turned away.

"Don't worry about me, Zach. FYI, I bench-press a-hundred-and-twenty pounds at the gym."

Surprise made him stop in his tracks. She looked like she hardly weighed a hundred and twenty pounds. He had to get over his stun when she exited the office and went to the entrance lobby. He followed after grabbing his damp jacket from the kitchen, slinging it over an arm.

"Give me the keys," he told her at the door. "I can close for you."

She smiled and handed him the keys, and for a second, he wanted to bask in this evident trust she had in him.

He was deceiving her, but she trusted him.

Suddenly, he felt like an abject arsehole.

Shrugging off the unpleasant feeling, he gave her the keys back and escorted her to her car.

"Open the back door for me, will you?" she asked.

He frowned. "You don't lock your car?"

"In my own parking? Nope."

Reckless of her.

She pushed the carrier onto the back seat and secured it with the seat belt, then closed the door and opened the driver's side. A frown touched her forehead, and Zach found himself stepping forward to figure out what had made her have this reaction.

He saw it then—the key was still in the ignition. And when she slid in and tried to start the car, nothing happened. Her hand went to the right side lever.

"*Merde!*" she cursed.

"What's the matter?" he asked.

She grimaced. "Guess who the idiot is that left the tail lights on and drained the battery on her car." She smacked the steering wheel. "*Mais quelle conasse, quand même!*"

He seemed to recall seeing a layer of fog on the surroundings of Balaclava this morning. Could be why she'd had the tail lights on. But she had forgotten to turn them off. Not to add how she had also left the key in the ignition, and never mind that she didn't lock her car at the office.

A niggling feeling assailed him and settled into his psyche like a splinter. Something didn't add up in this scenario. He'd seen her work, and coupled with Wexler's report on her professional life, both had both shown him how she was a conscientious and efficient agency director. He would never have imagined she could be scatter-brained.

In the distance, they could hear the rumble of thunder once more. The cats. She should get them home.

"Let's take my car," he said. "I can drop you at your place and bring you back tomorrow after we've found jump cables or something."

She sighed. "They did warn me at the last servicing the car would need a new battery soon. Best I get a new one. Tomorrow, though. Everywhere will be closed today."

He waved towards his Jag. "Come on."

She nodded and opened the back door to grab the carrier. Loulou was still howling. With the car doors closed, he had hardly heard the cat.

Annabelle thanked him once inside his SUV, and the animal kept up his long-suffering litany all the way to Balaclava.

"How do you know this is where I live?" she asked.

Damn. He should've covered his back better. "When I mentioned the agency had set me up in a hotel here, someone at the office said you also lived in the region."

"Of course," she said with a laugh. "Never tell that lot anything you want to remain on the down low, by the way."

"I'll keep it in mind." He slowed the car at a junction in the road. "So, where to?"

"Take a left here, then left again at the side road under the dark canopy of trees."

He took the direction and got them onto the specific road. "You like it here?"

"It's home."

He threw her a quizzical look.

"Let me rephrase that. It's quiet, close to the beach, and the people, though they do follow your every move and know all your business, well, they tend to keep to themselves, and you're thus spared from being accountable for your every step."

"Good neighbourly values and all that," he joked.

"Exactly." She laughed. "See, the Range Rover in front of Mrs. DaSilva's house? Probably her new beau. And the blonde Barbie-lookalike over there with the pram? That's the fifth nanny since the Harleys settled a few houses down a year ago. It is said Mr. Harley loves them young and blonde, especially now his wife is no longer either."

Zach chuckled along, but inside, he bit his cheek. He'd have to get Jonathan to move the Range Rover. His associate had just been made. Who would've thought such a quiet neighbourhood would have such eagle-eyed occupants that would make spies look like brainless dimwits? The luxury vehicle should've blended into this posh neighbourhood.

He stopped the Jag at her gate, and she lowered the window and aimed a fob at the keypad on the side. The portal started sliding open, and he sped the vehicle through and braked in front of her sprawling one-storey concrete and glass residence.

"Nice place," he said.

She laughed. "Come, I'll give you the tour. The least I can do to thank you is offer you a cup of coffee."

He alighted from the Jag and opened the back door before she could. "Allow me to get that for you. I suppose your house is locked when you're not there."

"Cheeky," she threw over her shoulder as she went to the front door.

Once she had opened it and secured the alarm, he grabbed the carrier, closed the car door with his elbow, and carried the surprisingly heavy thing inside. The second he put it down and Annabelle gave him the thumbs up to open the latch after she had closed the front door, Loulou's howls stopped as if by a miracle, and the grey-and-black-striped little monster was the first one out to go hide under a sofa in the living room. Fifi came out next, hobbling on his one front paw, Riri at his back as if to keep an eye on him.

"Finally, you're back!" a voice said in crisp English.

Zach straightened, all his senses going on high alert. There was a man here. Annabelle lived with someone?

How had he not known this? And who was the bastard who got to put his dirty paws on her?

At the flare of red-hot jealousy spearing through him, he closed his eyes for a second and forced himself to return to a better countenance. Annabelle could be with someone—Zach didn't own her or anything. They were nothing, the two of them. Not even friends.

And as long as he couldn't prove she wasn't Evangeline, she would remain his mark. He shouldn't forget it.

With a deep breath, he followed her into the house. Around the bend stood a ladder against the wall. A tall, buff man who looked like a modern Viking with his massive build and blond hair and beard was carefully easing an abstract canvas into place on the wall.

"There," the man said and stepped back down to look at his work.

"Lars!" Annabelle chided.

Okay, definitely Scandinavian, then. She had an expat boyfriend they didn't know about?

"What are you doing here?" she continued.

"Since there was no work today, Simmi told me to come over and help you with those paintings."

"You didn't have to—"

"I did." The man cut her exasperated spiel without even looking at her. "You fell off the ladder and hit your head last week, and my wife and I had to get up in the middle of the night to take you to Casualty."

She grumbled something in reply, but Zach wasn't listening to her. No, he was still focused on the words this Lars had said.

The man noticed him then, and his eyes narrowed. Zach recognised the look for what it was because he glared at every one of Zenobia's male friends the same way. This guy had Annabelle's back. Good.

He inched forward and put his hand out. "Zach Hashemi. A business colleague of Annabelle's."

The Viking eyed him with his narrowed gaze for long seconds, then he clasped the offered hand and shook it with a powerful, almost crushing grip. Zach totally got the message.

"Lars Rutherford," he said. "Simmi, my wife, is Annabelle's cousin."

They both dropped their hands, though one could still cut the tension between them with a knife. Annabelle seemed oblivious to the crackling energy in the room and took a turn into the open plan kitchen.

"Nespresso, everyone?" she asked.

"Yes," they both replied.

Zach recalled the man's words from before they were introduced, and he edged closer so Annabelle wouldn't hear him.

"So, she fell off this ladder?" he asked.

Lars frowned, then his eyebrows relaxed as if he had decided he could trust Zach even just a little bit. "Yep."

"Is she always this accident-prone?"

"Annabelle? A tsunami wouldn't be able to make her budge. The woman is a force of Nature all on her own." Lars shook his head. "That's why we were so surprised when we heard she had fallen." He paused. "My wife also thinks she took a tumble down the stairs at our house the other day, but she keeps denying it."

Zach wondered why the man was confiding in him so much. One thing he had to acknowledge: Lars sounded deeply worried about her.

And Zach couldn't fault him that. In fact, he was grateful someone had noticed something. Annabelle had lost her balance and had fallen twice when she never seemed to have had any problem with equilibrium before. Add to it the fact that she had been consistently forgetful recently.

As the picture started to form in his head, horror iced the blood in his veins. Because if he was right, she was either developing a neurological condition at her young age, or someone was introducing neurotoxins into her environment so she'd slowly but surely go off her rocker.

He knew of only one person who loved to play this kind of twisted game. Evangeline.

Could Annabelle have become her latest mark?

He better alert Alexis as soon as possible. They might have had this wrong the whole time!

***

Balaclava, Mauritius.
Saturday, February 7. 1.47 p.m.

An exhausted Annabelle trudged back home. The dealership had managed to send someone to the office with a new battery for her car, and staying around to make sure it was taken care of had eaten into her work time. With Daniel away, it all fell onto her shoulders, and coupled with the early afternoon she'd had to take the previous day, she was way behind on her work. On top of setting up Margot's pop-up store idea, the launch for Avignon was drawing closer, too.

But she couldn't think of this now. Lately, she'd been functioning under a sort of brain fog throwing a dampener on all her senses. She cringed as she recalled how she had fallen off the ladder last week, and the tumble she had taken down Simmi's stairs the day before. What was happening to her? Overworking herself? It didn't help that she also had to worry about the magnifying lens Wexler-Prinsloo had put on them through Zach.

She frowned as she thought of him. He had seemed ... off with her today. It had felt like coddling, but why would he coddle her? Unless Lars had opened his big mouth and told him about her recent woes. The man really didn't know how to mind his own business sometimes.

Still, she had left all this behind now. She would take this afternoon off, catch up on some Netflix binge-watching with some wine later. But first, a swim. The thunderstorm of yesterday had marked the start of the torrential rains period. For the past couple of years, almost every day in February, the sky would grow lead-grey around eleven a.m., and the dams would burst around one p.m., the rains keeping at it sometimes until three.

It was already close to two o'clock—seemed like their region had been spared the downpour today. She could sneak in a long swim that would allow her to clear the cobwebs from her mind. Exercise always did it for her, swimming even more as being under the water was akin to being in another world in a meditative state.

So after ditching her work clothes and getting into a bikini, she went out to the deck at the back, plunging into the pool with hardly a splash.

The water surrounded her, her hearing growing muffled, her eyes stinging a little from the chlorine. Her body stopped resisting, and the buoyancy took her, making her let go. Ah, how good this felt. She swam to the bottom, made it up top for another gulp of air, and repeated this over and over.

She had her feet on the concrete floor when she noticed the water around her had grown darker like there was no more sun. As she looked up, it was to find big drops of rain pattering on the pool water. Within a few seconds, she couldn't see the surface—the rain had turned into a downpour already.

But something stranger caught her attention. Light, lots of it. Orange. Unnatural. It seemed to converge on all sides of the pool.

She squinted. What the hell …

With a quick push down on the floor, she propelled her body through the water and broke the surface. What she saw had her eyes open wide with terror and horror. Fire. A raging inferno, blazing all around the pool. She turned and turned, looking for a way out, but there was none. The flames had eaten every inch of the deck, and it seemed they were starting to lick at the glass panes of the sliding doors leading inside.

The cats! Had she closed the doors when she'd come out? Would they be able to escape? Fifi wouldn't be able to run …

A panicked gasp escaped her as she twirled around, still trying to find a way out. Her throat clenched, and she coughed to ease her trachea. However, this only made it worse. The more she coughed, the less air she was able to take in. Her eyes were also burning, and there was a strange smell in the air, like the stinging stink of ammonia-laden cheap hair dye. What could it be? She had to get out …

But she couldn't, and soon, it became harder to keep herself afloat as the coughing intensified and her eyes went so blurry, she couldn't make out anything but vague shapes and specks of colour.

A part of her reckoned it, though she was loath to face it—this was death. She wouldn't make it out of this pool. Her darling cats would also die in the fire; rescue services wouldn't have time to come around to save them.

There was so much she still had in her, so much she wanted to do. Alas, she wouldn't be able to.

Like going for the teacup ride at one of those fairy-tale themed parks. Eating gelato again on a bench in Rome. Swim with the dolphins off the West coast of Mauritius—she'd always said she'd do it one day.

She wouldn't get the chance now.

One day, she'd also thought she would find love … and lately, that fantasy had placed Zach's likeness in the position of the usually faceless man she had with her as she visualized her ideal life.

Zach … In another world, under other circumstances …

She'd never know now. When the burn in her throat stopped her from being able to take in air, she surrendered and closed her eyes.

Zach's face was the last thing she saw before darkness claimed her.

CHAPTER FIVE

Balaclava, Mauritius.
Saturday, February 7. 2.15 p.m.

The smell of burning chemicals assaulted Zach's nostrils as soon as he stepped onto Annabelle's property. Damn it, this was bad. As luck would have it, he'd been in Jonathan's Range Rover outside on the road when the smoke had appeared on top of her back garden. In his line of work, smoke raised alarm bells, so he'd listened to his instincts screaming at him that something terrible was happening and had barged into her yard. During recon, they'd found the alarm covered the house only, not the entire courtyard. So jumping over the gate had been easy.

He rushed to the side of the dwelling—the smoke seemed to be coming from out back. As he turned onto the paved pathway, the stench of ammonia and something like drain cleaner hit him square on, and he lifted his shirt and used the edge to cover his nose and mouth. Someone coughed behind him—good, Jonathan had followed him.

When he emerged into the garden at the back, he froze. The smoke came from a fire burning all around the pool. Annabelle. Where was she? He'd followed her home earlier, and he now prayed she was inside and safe from the flames for the time being. The blaze was burning steadily despite the rain, and this made him frown. Such a downpour should've prevented a fire in the first place and would have extinguished it within a few minutes.

Something wasn't sitting right in his gut … and as he jumped onto the three-foot wall bordering the raised flower beds along the edges, a fleck of black caught his attention in the pool. He squinted, frowned, and then cursed aloud when he made out someone trying to break the surface of the water, struggling to get their head out. Annabelle. Her thick hair had fanned all around her, hence him picking up on the black colour. Against the roar of the flames, the sounds she was making as she struggled to stay afloat were hardly registering in the air.

"She's in the water!" he yelled at Jonathan.

The other man nodded, and before Zach could leap from the wall, he pulled a now-soaked towel that had been drying on the clothesline and threw it over the concrete bordering the pool.

Good idea—the towel would snuff the fire and allow a path to the pool.

"What the hell," Jonathan cursed as the fire burst onto the towel and started burning even harder.

"Water-reactive explosives," Zach suddenly said as the notion dawned and horror flooded him in its wake.

He threw a quick glance around. Nothing but the concrete deck around the freeform pool was burning—it must be where the chemicals were. If the rain hadn't started falling … He shuddered at the thought. Annabelle … He had to get her out of the water. She had probably passed out from the fumes.

His gaze landed on a plastic lounge chair farther down on the lawn. Without thinking twice, he rushed to it, grabbed it, and, before throwing it over the fire burning on the closest edge of the pool, he twisted and sent his own body flying into the air, hurtling down with the lounger like on a body board to land with a splash in the pool. Fire blazed where the water hit it.

But he couldn't care about that, nor about the sting on his left shoulder as that side of his body soared closest to the flames. Once in the water, he kicked and tread up, breaking the surface next to Annabelle's body. He made quick work of lifting her torso out of the water and tugging her to his chest. With a frantic hand, he reached for her neck and felt for a pulse.

There. Faint, but there. A sigh of relief rushed out of him as he kicked on with his legs to keep them both afloat. He could also feel her breath fanning his neck. She hadn't ingested water into her lungs, then. They'd gotten here just in time.

"Is she alive?" Jonathan yelled from the garden.

"Just barely. We have to get her out of the water."

The two men looked around the place.

"Wait, I have an idea." Jonathan rushed to the side, under a wood awning with climbing plants on it, and grabbed a big white sack from under it. He then carried the bag over, ripped it open, and spread its contents on the concrete. The fire snuffed itself out as the potting soil landed on it.

"Clear a path!" Zach shouted.

"That's the plan," the other man said as he repeated the procedure.

Within a minute, he had extinguished the fire along one side of the pool and opened the way to the sliding doors of the house.

As soon as he saw the pathway, Zach pushed himself to the edge of the pool. Jonathan helped him pull Annabelle's body from the water, and he rushed to the door, sighing with relief when it slid open under his hand. She hadn't locked it when she'd come out to the pool. Jonathan had followed and placed Annabelle's body into Zach's arms.

"There are three cats inside the house," he told his partner. "Make sure they're safe after you get the fire under control."

"On it," Jonathan replied as he closed the door behind them.

Zach wasted no more time to rush inside to her bedroom, where the en-suite would be. With her still in his arms, he got into the shower cabin and started the waterfall spout on top. Cold water rained down and doused them. His skin erupted into Goosebumps, but he couldn't pay this any heed as he needed to get her cleaned ASAP. He had a feeling it had been potassium mixed with other compounds out there on the deck, igniting upon contact with water. Exposure to such chemicals required a safety shower within ten seconds of being around the substance. Annabelle had been exposed for much longer than that.

She still hadn't woken up, despite him keeping them under the shower for a count of five minutes in his head, and this had him worried. But he had more important things to take care of, like washing her eyes out because the fumes would've hurt them.

"I apologize for this," he mumbled as he left her under the shower and went to the sink, which he plugged, and then ran the tap. When the porcelain basin had filled with water, he went back for her, and loath as he was to do what he'd do next, he had no choice.

So he propped her against the counter, wrapped his grip around her hair, and then plunged her head into the water.

For a second or two, she didn't react. But then, she started to struggle, fighting him off.

He lifted her head to check if she had opened her eyes. She had—good. He plunged her back under. She kept on struggling, but he wrapped one leg around hers and kept her in place. When satisfied the chemical residue had been washed off her eyes, he released her and pulled her away.

She gasped and sputtered, then landed in a heap on the floor.

He started towards her, but a shadow in the doorway made him stop. He glanced up into Jonathan's too-serious face.

"You have to do it," the man told him.

Zach froze. There was no other way. He would have to bite the bullet.

So he nodded, and when Jonathan handed him the syringe, he didn't blink. Instead, he took a deep breath and went to her. She scrambled away from him, and the mere sight broke his heart. But he had no other choice. This was protocol, and he was a Corpus agent. She was a civilian who knew nothing of their clandestine world and its underhanded operations.

Grabbing her with a gentle hold, he stopped himself from flinching as he slammed the needle into her neck and pushed the plunger to release the sedative into her body. Three seconds later, she had gone limp in his arms.

A wave of nausea rose through his gorge. He bent over the commode and chucked bile out.

"Zach ..."

He quelled the shaking in his body as the adrenalin left him, and he looked up at the dark-haired man still on the threshold.

"You should put her to bed. A doctor will be here soon to check her out."

Jonathan was thinking clearly here, where he wasn't. True, the man had no tie or attachment to Annabelle. If this had been the woman *he* loved here—

Zach closed his eyes. No, not that notion. There was nothing between him and Annabelle. There couldn't be.

The sooner he accepted this reality and crystallized it into his every cell, the better. The shit had just hit the fan here. Everything had changed. They'd lost their grip on everything they'd thought to be the truth until now. They had to regroup, recover, and re-strategize.

"You spoke to Alexis?" Zach asked.

Jonathan nodded. "I've apprised her, yes."

Zach glanced at Annabelle, still on the marble floor next to him. Gently, he reached for her and cradled her body to his. He stood, grabbed a towel from the rack, and carried her into the adjoining room where he dried her off before placing her on the bed.

"Zach, did you hear me? Alexis said—"

"Not until I'm sure she's okay," he growled.

Jonathan blinked, but then nodded. "Man, you know what you're doing?"

He had no fucking clue, to be honest.

"She matters," he simply said.

"Of course. But she will be out for the next six to eight hours, at least. There's nothing more we can do for her until the doctor arrives. Alexis is also sending a crew to sweep the house and do a forensic clean up. So far, it seems the neighbours on both sides of her property are absent. We can fib the smoke as a barbecue attempt gone awry."

They should contain this incident—he knew it. At least, a part of him did, and he should heed said part.

Because he wouldn't be of any help to her until they figured out what the hell was going on.

He turned to cast a long look at her on the bed. Her chest rose and fell steadily, and she seemed for all intents and purposes merely asleep. But he knew how far from the truth that was.

Suddenly not able to take it, he whirled on his heel and stormed out of the room, slamming into the rock wall separating the living room area from this hallway and throwing his fist into the hard surface. Pain radiated from the point of contact, and instead of gritting his teeth to contain the emotions bubbling inside him, he pressed his forehead to the panel and let out a raging scream.

"Man, you're soaked through."

Zach sneered. See if he cared.

"You won't be of much help to her if you catch your death from pneumonia," Jonathan continued. Damn him, but he was right. "I've got my gym bag in the car. There's a change of clothes in there."

Zach peeled himself from the wall and turned to face his partner. "Thanks, man."

Jonathan nodded. "I'll go get it. By the way, the cats are fine. The grey and black striped one ducked under the sofa when it saw me. The other two were in the cat tree near the kitchen."

The cats. Of course, that anti-social monster of Loulou would go into hiding. He went into the living room and peered under the sofa. And right as he'd expected, the little shit hissed at him and tried to rip his eye out with his claws. Excellent—this must mean the chemicals had not affected his sunny disposition. Riri and Fifi were still casually lounging on the tree, tails slowly swishing as they watched him.

And speaking of the chemicals ... He took a turn towards the sliding doors, stopping there to gather the extent of the damage outside. The rain had turned into a fine drizzle, and the potting soil Jonathan had used to extinguish the fire had morphed into a dirty mire. The man had gone back to cover the entire perimeter of the pool with the earth. Thank goodness Annabelle's gardener had had these packets lying around.

Water-reactive explosives. He shuddered.

Who in their right mind would go for something as volatile and deadly?

From what he gathered looking at the burn trail, the stuff must've been deposited all around the pool. If it hadn't rained, no one would've been the wiser as to its presence. Someone who went into the pool wouldn't think twice about coming out and walking the concrete. Their wet feet would touch the chemicals, the water reacting with them, setting the soles on fire. The person would most probably lose their balance and fall, the rest of their wet body getting into contact with more explosives on the concrete deck. They would be on fire within a minute. A horrible, slow, and painful death.

Something which had been waiting for Annabelle ... Again, if the rain hadn't fallen while she'd still been in the water ...

He startled when Jonathan closed the front door. Zach reached for the clothes the man handed over, and he went back to the en-suite to ditch his wet garments, towel himself dry, then tug on the sweatpants and T-shirt. He and Jonathan were of similar height, but the man was way leaner. His T-shirt stuck to Zach like a fitted bodysuit. Still, it would do for the time being.

His hand started to sting—delayed reaction from all the adrenalin and roiling emotions, surely—and he noticed the torn knuckles on a few fingers. He made quick work of finding some antibiotic ointment and a roll of crepe bandage in the medicine cabinet, using them to attend to his wound and wrap his hand protectively.

As he stepped back into the bedroom, he quelled the urge to go to her, the un-bandaged hand closing into a tight fist as he restrained himself from flying over to her side on the king-size bed. He wouldn't be of any help to her until he had figured out what was happening.

So he gritted his teeth and exited the room, finding Jonathan in the spot he had vacated in front of the sliding doors.

"This was Evangeline's work," the man told him without turning around.

It wasn't a question—Jonathan had come to the same conclusion, too.

"Alexis is awaiting your call. I told her you had your hands full when I notified her earlier."

Zach nodded and went to the kitchen counter to sit down on a tall bar stool. The energy was leaving his body, rendering him weak and tired. But he had to power on.

He paused as he glanced around. To think that just yesterday, he'd been sitting at this same counter drinking coffee with Annabelle and Lars.

He shook the thought off and focused on the phone as he went through the hoops to call the boss. The video call burst to life less than a minute later; she seemed to be in the Prague facility, the imperial décor in the background a far cry from the minimalism of the Berlin office. The camera then panned out to include a dark man with long shaggy hair and intense emerald eyes. Graeme, her second in command.

"Jonathan told us about the fire," she started. "How is Annabelle?"

"We got here just in time. She's alive. I've had to sedate her, though."

She winced. "Protocol, of course. I'm sorry."

At least, there was that. He nodded. "So, what now?"

"We can pretty much ascertain she is not Evangeline. Annabelle doesn't fit the profile, based on your reports, Zachariah. And even if she had a death wish, she would not endanger her cats."

"She wouldn't," he concurred.

"Plus Gaia found a trail on the dark web—someone asking about a gun for hire to make a kill in Kinshasa around the same period Dax Vosloo was killed. They say they found no trace of any Dark-web connection on Annabelle's computer or her network at the office. No VPN or proxy servers used to mask her trails, either. According to them, she is a virtual open book."

Gaia was a duo of elite hackers behind the Corpus security net and their entire communications framework. If they hadn't been able to find anything, then there was nothing to uncover.

Zach gulped as the idea solidified in his mind. "Evangeline is now after her."

Alexis nodded. "It would seem like it. Is Jonathan around? Can he hear me?"

"He's right here." Zach waved the man over.

"Good. Because the mission has now changed, gentlemen. You're still there to find Evangeline, but we also have a civilian in her crosshairs. You will be protecting Annabelle de Castelban until this assassin is apprehended."

"Roger that," they both said.

A beep resounded from the entryway. Jonathan went to investigate.

"The crew is here," he called out.

"I'll leave you to your work, then," Alexis said. "Contact me if there's anything."

"Yes, ma'am."

She cut the call before anyone else could enter the room. No one but a trusted few of her agents knew of her role as the head of the Corpus.

Zach pocketed the phone then went to the door. Men in coveralls were exiting the van, and they made their way to the back and got started on cleaning up the pool area. To anyone looking, it would seem like they were resurfacing the concrete deck.

An older man and a young woman, both with a doctor's satchel in hand, entered the house. Jonathan directed the man to the bedroom while the woman noticed the cats on the tree and went to them. Zach frowned. So Alexis had also despatched a veterinarian to check on the animals? It was generous and unexpected of her.

He took in a deep breath as he scanned the scene around him. They had way too many questions and not enough answers. Starting with how much the chemicals could've affected Annabelle. From what he remembered, water-reactive chemicals were extremely toxic and could damage the liver, kidney, reproductive system, and the central nervous system. Until Annabelle woke up …

He closed his eyes tight for a second, unable to even think of anything irreversible happening to her. This was all his fault. If he'd told Alexis about his suspicions sooner, if he'd trusted his gut when it told him Annabelle wasn't a killer, if he hadn't convinced himself that this feeling came from him pulling the wool over his eyes because he was attracted to her, none of this would've happened. He would've stuck to her like white on rice and protected her.

A small, humourless chuckle escaped him as he thought of those words. White on rice—her nickname for him.

Would he ever hear her laugh again? See the mischievous sparkle in her eyes?

A hissed growl tore him out of his doldrums, and he rolled his eyes and cursed. Of course, Loulou was being a diva again. The poor vet seemed to have her hands full trying to catch the tabby so she could look him over.

Zach went over to the sofa. With a swift push, he moved the piece of furniture then swooped down to catch the cat unawares. But the little brat retaliated, scratching Zach's forearms with his back legs and twisting his head to the side to bite Zach's wrist.

He cursed under his breath and was grateful to surrender the feral animal to the vet who pinned him down with expert placement of her left hand on his neck, three fingers over his head, thumb and pinkie under the ears. Surprisingly, Loulou remained flattened that way on the sofa as the vet managed to take a look at him. But the second she released his head, he jumped off and rushed into the bedroom, a gargled rumble sounding as though he were cursing them the only indication of where he'd gone.

The vet turned startled eyes onto Zach. "You must have your hands full with him."

"I ..." *He's not my cat*, he wanted to say. But he had no idea how much she knew, so best he played this safe. "You don't know the half of it."

And he wasn't lying or stretching the truth by saying that. Loulou was indeed a handful. How Annabelle coped, he had no idea.

And speaking of her … He should go check on her. So with a deep breath to fortify his resolve, he started towards her bedroom.

The doctor was removing the butterfly needle to take blood samples from her elbow. He looked up when Zach came in.

"I'll know more once I have these tested." He rattled the blood-filled tubes in his hand.

The man spoke with a German accent. Zach frowned. Alexis having sent him, could he also be a member of their agency?

The doctor laughed softly. "I can see the gears clicking. Yes, I work for her, too. I was her teacher for a long time."

Before she took on the mantle of the head of the Corpus, Alexis had been the agency's medical doctor. It was starting to make sense now.

Zach stopped by the bed. "How is she?"

"For the moment, stable. Your partner is getting the portable oxygen from the van as we speak. Until she wakes up, we won't know what damage the fumes have wrought on her nervous system, but physically, right now, the biggest risk is her developing pulmonary oedema after being exposed to the ammonia in the fumes. Oxygen therapy should help with that."

"She'll need to be monitored?" Zach asked.

"Definitely." The doctor nodded as Jonathan came in with an oxygen tank and all the associated paraphernalia, and proceeded to set the whole thing up. With gentle care, he then placed the nasal cannula on her face and let her head loll back onto the pillow.

"Someone should dry her hair and get her into warmer clothes. Her lungs don't need pneumonia on top of everything."

Jonathan looked to Zach, who nodded in reply to the silent question. Yes, he was the one who would be taking care of her.

As the two men exited the room, he went to the bed and got down on his knees. She looked so peaceful there as she slept. But she wasn't just sleeping, he reminded himself. She had been exposed to chemicals from water-reactive explosives, had almost died, then he'd knocked her out cold with the sedative injection.

He hadn't taken good enough care of her ... And that was changing now, he vowed as he clenched his jaw.

Getting to his feet, he went to the wardrobe where he looked for something comfortable and warm to get her into. He cursed as he went through the racks and drawers. What sort of woman didn't own any loungewear? His sister swore she'd live in those if she could. Finally finding an oversize T-shirt and a pair of exercise leggings, he took those with him.

At the bed, he forced himself to blank his mind as he removed the scraps of the bikini on her and got her into the clothes. The T-shirt went first, doing a fine enough job of covering her nudity. He continued to blank his senses as he rolled the leggings over her limbs. They'd have to do—he was not taking the risk of putting underwear on her. Next, he went in search of the hair dryer, and after having plugged it into a socket near the bedside table, proceeded to dry her voluminous hair.

Time stopped as he focused on this task. When finally satisfied her hair was fully dry, he shut down the device and let it fall to the floor.

"Zach, food," Jonathan said from the door.

"Not until she wakes up," he muttered.

He wouldn't be able to think of anything until he knew she was safe. The other man took the hint and didn't bother him anymore.

Zach must've have dozed off at some point. He woke up to find Jonathan shaking his shoulder where he'd fallen into a heap against the bedside table. His eyes grew wide as he registered the people in white plastic coveralls in the hallway, two of them entering the bedroom.

"What's going on?" he croaked.

Jonathan shook his head. "It's bad, man. Dr. Berger called. He found high levels of Varden in Annabelle's blood."

Everything inside him froze, his stomach however twisting and surging forth with bile. Zach quelled it before he upchucked his guts on the floor or on Jonathan who was crouched in front of him.

As Corpus agents, they both knew what the name implied. They say people who deal with death dealers had a macabre sense of humour. This couldn't apply more to Varden, a proprietary neurotoxin the Corpus had developed in its labs in Geneva. The name actually came from the expression *'verrückt werden'* in German—literally meaning 'to go crazy.' Because it's what Varden did to the people exposed to it.

The one condition Varden needed to work was time—the longer the exposure, the more damage it could wreak.

This would explain why Annabelle had been getting forgetful lately, why she had lost her balance on at least two occasions he knew of, and fell. The neurotoxin had already started doing its job, which meant it must have been in her system for a while.

For definitely way more than the one-week-or-so since Dax Vosloo had given them her name in Kinshasa.

Evangeline must've been after her for some time already. And if he thought of it, Vosloo had turned to the Corpus some four weeks earlier, when he had cut from his partner and betrayed her. Evangeline must've been playing her game on two fronts—targeting Vosloo on one, getting rid of Annabelle on the other. Vosloo's death had been quick, from a gun for hire. Annabelle's would've been slow and painful, precisely the kind the twisted assassin loved to set up and watch unfold.

Evangeline was here, close to Annabelle.

And the fire had been a precipitated attempt to kill her already, before the Corpus could get to the information Vosloo must've given her, probably without her knowledge. He and Jonathan must have been made.

Zach jumped to his feet as the pieces of the puzzle clicked into place. However, before he could tell Jonathan anything, the sensor that looked like a lit-up TV remote in the suit's hand started beeping near the bed. As the man got closer to the headboard, the beeps became a persistent screech. The guy turned the device off, pulled a piece of paper-like strip from his pocket which he placed on the fabric of the headboard. The strip went red.

The Varden was in the headboard.

"Take her out! Get away from here!" he told them.

"Damn it! She would have been exposed every night for ten hours straight under this thing," Zach threw out as he reached for her, dislodged the nasal cannula, and pulled her into his arms.

"*J'ai l'antidote avec moi,*" a woman told him from the hallway.

She had the antidote, she'd said in French. Dr. Berger must've figured out the levels of the poison in her blood. If he'd sent the remedy over, this meant she could still be saved.

He wasted no time following her into the living room where he placed Annabelle on the sofa. The woman converged onto them with a syringe filled with a Curaçao-blue liquid. After tying some rubber tubing tight on Annabelle's upper arm, she then tapped the hollow of her elbow to find the vein. The needle went in next, the blue antidote dislodging itself into her bloodstream.

The woman removed the syringe and the rubber band then looked up at him. "She'll need another dose in twenty hours, given her exposure. Can you give an intravenous shot?"

He nodded. He'd learned how during his training.

"Good," she said. "Give me your hand."

"Why?" He frowned.

She rolled her eyes and grabbed his hand. Before he could reckon what was happening, a sharp prick lanced the pad of his thumb. He cursed. When a little ball of blood formed, she touched it with the tip of a strip attached to a hand-held device.

"You weren't exposed for long enough to warrant needing the antidote." She glanced around the place. "So far, we've been able to ascertain the only Varden nest was in the headboard of her bed."

Targeting her for maximum exposure, because she spent the major part of the night close to said headboard, sleeping. This had definitely been a twisted and macabre assassination attempt that had taken a lot of planning.

But why Annabelle? Could it be jealousy, because Vosloo had been with her in the past? From what Zach had gathered, Vosloo would be leaving Annabelle's bed to go grace Evangeline's. Why hadn't the killer gotten her knickers in a twist then?

No, there must be something about Annabelle she feared.

Movement next to him tore him out of his thoughts.

The woman reached over and ran a gentle finger over Annabelle's forehead, tucking a lock of hair away. "The levels of the toxin in her blood were high, but you got to her just in time for the antidote to work."

Thank God for that. He sighed with pent-up relief.

Then, he frowned. The antidote was another one of Alexis' despatches. How had the woman gotten it here this fast? Had the boss known something?

"How did you get here so quickly?"

"We're based next door," she said. "Réunion."

Réunion Island was a French DOM-TOM, an overseas department in the Indian Ocean, and Mauritius' closest neighbour. They operated under French and European law—no wonder the Corpus also had a facility there, which would explain it all. It would take someone just forty-five minutes on a plane to hop from one island to the other. Alexis hadn't known. He didn't know what he'd do if he'd found out he couldn't trust the woman who had all their lives in her hand.

"Hey, you," the Frenchwoman cooed as Fifi approached the sofa.

The cats. Had they been exposed, too?

"Do they need to be tested?" he asked.

She shook her head. "The beauty of Varden is how it only works on the human nervous system."

Hearing this gave him the creeps. He reached over before she could touch Fifi and held the little cat protectively against his stomach.

She gave him a knowing smile as she got up and patted the small black case she had left on the coffee table. "Second shot. Twenty hours."

She left, the rest of the crew following after her. Zach put Fifi down on the floor, then took a turn into the bedroom. He winced when he saw the wide gap where they had uprooted the headboard from the wall. Annabelle would have his gut for garters.

He returned in front. Jonathan closed the front door and let his body drop onto a sofa once he reached the living room.

"You weren't exposed?" the man asked.

"Not enough time," Zach replied. "You?"

"Same thing." Jonathan brought his hands up and ran them over his face and into his hair. "The neurotoxin must have been there for weeks."

He had figured that out, too. Evangeline had come for her with Varden. What had pushed the assassin to use the water-reactive compound? She loved to wait for the long game, usually.

Unless her time was running out.

Two things he now knew for sure: Evangeline loved to watch her prey die a slow death; she must be around somewhere. And second, she wouldn't have come after Annabelle so strongly if she didn't need her dead quickly.

What about Annabelle had put her on the death list of the dedicated killer so badly?

Could it have anything to do with Dax Vosloo's parting words?

He gulped as he looked at her on the sofa. She *must* know something. The key to bringing Evangeline down surely rested with her.

He glanced up at Jonathan. "Are you thinking what I'm thinking?"

Jonathan took a deep breath then sighed. "You have to bring her in on this operation."

CHAPTER SIX

Balaclava, Mauritius
Sunday, February 8. 5.29 p.m.

Annabelle tore herself from a deep slumber. She stretched out, and with her eyes still closed, could hear the sound of rain pattering outside as the drops hit the surface of the pool.

A lance of pain registered on her arm, and she winced and tried to pull away from it. But it only hurt more, and her eyes flew open to stare at ... someone injecting something into her vein? What the hell? And who ...? Her mouth dropped, a silent cry forcing itself out of her burning throat as her gaze landed on Zach.

"What the ..." she croaked.

"Easy," he soothed. "It's okay. I got you."

In what world did he think she would believe such bullshit? A man didn't drug a woman unless he wanted to do dirty and despicable things to her when she was passed out.

"Get away from me!" she shouted.

At least, she thought she shouted because the words came out a raspy murmur bringing on a fit of coughing.

"Here," he coaxed, placing something over her mouth.

Instinct told her to get away, to dislodge whatever he'd put on her face, but as she tried doing just that, she ended up breathing in from the contraption, and this eased the burn in her chest a little bit.

Wait, so this wasn't hurting her? She slammed his hand away from the oxygen mask—she recognized it for what it was when she placed her palm over it—and proceeded to take deep breaths until her throat felt a lot less sore.

When she could swallow without feeling like her trachea had been rubbed raw by sandpaper, she dislodged the mask from her mouth and lowered it to the sofa.

She frowned. What was she doing on the sofa? She hated falling asleep on it because she always ended up with a bad crick in her neck afterwards. And there was this matter of Zach injecting her with something. The bloody pervert. Why had he drugged her?

"Get out," she growled at him.

He sat with his arse propped on the coffee table, his worried gaze on her.

Why was he worried? Because his drug of choice hadn't worked on her, that she was still conscious? And what the hell was he even doing here? She hadn't invited him into her house, as far as she recalled. She had come here after leaving the office and had gone for a swim. Then ...

An image straight from a nightmare materialized in her mind—fire everywhere, smoke, a burning stench, water tugging her down—and she heard someone wailing from afar.

But it wasn't *someone*. It was *her* crying out that way like a frail, wounded animal.

Next, she was wrapped tight in Zach's arms, and he was rocking her like she were a little kid.

"It's okay," he mumbled. "You're safe now. I won't let anything happen to you."

She blinked, forcing her eyes open when closing them brought the sights of that hellish apocalypse to assail her once again.

His big body was tense against hers, his grip reeking of an emotion striking her remarkably like desperation. What ... Why ...? He was holding her like he would never let go.

"Zach? What happened?" she asked when the memory of the blaze slammed itself into her again. She had been in the water, dying ... then she recalled seeing his face before the darkness wrapped her in its clutches.

Suddenly, she shrugged herself out of his grip and jumped from the sofa to go to the sliding doors. Nothing seemed out of place outside—had this fire been her imagination at play? The cats, all three of them, were in the cat tree either asleep or lounging around, even Loulou who never liked to share his spot with any other cat. A glance at her outfit showed her in an old T-shirt and a pair of leggings. And her hair. What had happened to it? It felt dry and stiff and bouffant as if she had failed to go through the rigorous routine of conditioner then mask then oil bath to tame the frizz.

Annabelle blinked. The cats were playing nice; she was in loungewear with no care about her appearance; Zach had been holding on to her; her hair was in its natural state ... That was it. She must have died, and this was the version of Heaven her soul had conjured for her. She wasn't a religious person, though she considered herself spiritual, and the science of consciousness as she conceived of it told her Heaven was simply a perfect rendition of what the living mind had aspired to.

She blinked again as she stared at Zach, who had stood from his seat. Strange how he, too, was dressed in sweatpants and a too-tight T-shirt. She didn't mind the snug garment moulding his well-defined pecs like a second skin, but the sweats? Couldn't her idea of Heaven have had her man in a GQ-cover-worthy suit, or better yet, his birthday suit?

Then, her glance landed on the small, opened black case on the coffee table, and everything inside her froze. Because the syringe with a few drops of a bright blue liquid still in its tube, the long, thin needle capped off, lay right there for all to see.

She looked up at him, squinting when she had to travel her gaze so far up. Since when had Zach been this tall? Oh, right, she was barefoot here.

"Am I tripping?" she asked him.

He sighed and shook his head. "Unfortunately, no."

"Am I dead?"

"Thank God, no!"

She blinked and shook her head, confusion assailing her. "This isn't making any sense."

He sighed, then reached her side in two steps to place gentle hands on her shoulders. Try as she wanted, she couldn't shake him off, a sort of numb, muddled fog having fallen over her.

"Why were you drugging me?" she asked.

Guess she was one of those dim-witted women who didn't know when they had to cut and run when danger seemed to be lurking around her in the form of a man—why else would she be looking for a rational explanation here?

He lowered his face to peer into hers. "You were poisoned."

"What?"

Even her legs seemed to be asking the question, as they sapped from under her. If he hadn't been holding her, she would've crumbled to the floor.

He quickly directed her back to the sofa and gently deposited her onto it.

"Damn it, you're not going under again!" he barked at her as he started shaking her softly.

But his words were in vain, and she did go under. In a way, she was grateful for the abyss when it opened itself up to claim her.

When she came to next, the living room was bathed in darkness broken by the glow of one sconce lit on the far wall. As she tugged herself upright, cobwebs started breaking away in her mind; she was having a hard time finding clarity to make sense of what was going on around her.

A throat cleared itself, the sound coming from the side, and she jerked around to find a tall, dark-haired man sitting at the kitchen island. Her first impression, once she got past the surprise, was that he wasn't dangerous. The crooked smile rang sincere, echoing the kindness in his dark blue eyes.

"Coffee?" he asked.

She shook her head to clear it. "Wouldn't say no."

Maybe this was a dream, and the coffee would wake her. She got up, her body feeling leaden and sore, and trudged to the island where she slid onto a stool.

"Who are you?" she asked.

Might as well start talking to her delusions. Her mind sure knew how to conjure them—he was an above-average handsome man when seen from up close.

"Jonathan."

She nodded. "I'm Annabelle."

"I know," he said with a full-on crooked grin now. "Here's your coffee."

Something glimmered on his left hand as he pushed the Nespresso cup her way. The glint of metal—a wedding ring. Perfect. Her hussy mind was inventing a married man for her to ogle now.

"I'm Zach's partner," he added.

She frowned. This wasn't part of the fantasy. Her fanfic mind did not go to slash, typically.

"You two need to talk," Jonathan said, looking over her shoulder.

When she turned, it was to find Zach standing there in a pair of dark wash jeans and a button-down shirt. It was the most casual she had ever seen him. No, wait, hadn't he been in sweats and a tight top earlier?

By the time she had dislodged the fuzziness in her brain, Zach had swapped places with Jonathan at the island. The other man had gone outside—she could see the top of his chestnut locks peeking from behind one of the loungers in the garden.

And speaking of the garden, and the pool, and the deck …

"I had the weirdest dream," she told Zach.

He cocked an eyebrow as he took a sip of the coffee Jonathan had left for him.

"It started raining when I was in the pool, and then, fire blazed everywhere. I closed my eyes, and when I woke up, it was to find you …" She gulped, unable to bring herself to say the words. "Never mind. I don't want you to think I come up with all sort of psycho stuff in my mind."

"No, go on. Tell me."

Was it her imagination, or had she heard something like worry in the deep rumble of his voice?

She rolled her eyes at the ceiling. "Okay, fine. I woke up to find you were slipping me something."

His nostrils flared, and he released his grip on his cup. "It wasn't a dream."

Annabelle reeled back at his soft words. He had to be joking, right? Nothing outside looked amiss, and he … Well, come to think of it, what was he doing here in her house? Based on the light through the window, it was close to dawn.

"What do you mean?" she found herself asking.

Like that was the real question she should be asking right now.

"Let me tell you a little story, okay?"

She stared at him, eyes boggling. If that's how he wanted to play it … There was a fifty-pound kettlebell in the cupboard against her feet under the island. She could slip down, open the door, grab the weight, and fling it at him within five seconds if he thought to try anything funny with her.

Her heart started racing, but she forced herself to regulate her breathing, waiting for him to deliver his story.

"So, there was this guy. A total low-life jerk. But even low-life jerks can have their uses. He became the right-hand man of a woman, a stone-cold psychopath who put her twisted talents up for grabs to the highest bidder as an assassin for hire."

She shivered as he told her this story. Where were they here? Inside a Lee Child or James Patterson thriller or something?

"Now, that part of his life was his secret identity," Zach continued. "In his other life, the everyday one, he met a woman and got into a relationship with her. But the assassin wouldn't let him loose when he fell in love with this woman, and he knew how once you'd gotten into such a secret, crime-filled life, there was no way out."

She found herself unwittingly enraptured by the tale. "So, what did he do?"

"He went with the assassin, left the other woman behind."

Strange, but she was feeling some empathy for the other woman, having been dumped with no excuse or anything like that, too.

"He continued doing the assassin's dirty work. Then, one day, his conscience must've made itself known more loudly. He decided to do the right thing and turned himself over to the authorities to help bring the killer down. Which enraged the psychopath. Nobody got away with leaving her. So she painted a target on the man's back and set out to make the other woman die a slow and painful death while she watched from the shadows."

Zach paused after this last line, and she gazed at him and shrugged. What was he getting at? This would be the perfect plot for a normal-heroine-in-abnormal-extraordinary-circumstances psychological thriller that was all the rage right now.

"The assassin's name is Evangeline. The man's name was Dax. Dax Vosloo."

Horror iced the blood in Annabelle's veins. This had to be a joke. He couldn't have said the name of the man who had abandoned her a year earlier without a word and who had fallen off the face of the Earth without a trace.

Dax's desertion had hurt, more from the abandonment itself rather than a broken heart—a part of her had always known the relationship between her and the Afrikaner was fun and games and nothing rolling towards the long haul.

"The other woman in the tale is you, Annabelle."

Wait, hold on one second. Time out. She jumped down from her stool and started pacing the space between the island and the sofa.

"Fuck this. I am not the type of woman who gets embroiled in this kind of far-fetched conspiracy tale. Who do you think me to be? An Ian Fleming ingénue heroine?"

"What?" He shook his head and left the island, too. "Never mind. What I'm trying to say here, Annabelle, is your life is in danger. Evangeline is coming after you. We know it now."

"We?" Her eyebrows must be touching her hairline by this point.

"It's not important—"

"Damn right it is!"

"Not now, Annabelle. Listen to me—"

If all this were true, if it hadn't been a dream, as he had said ...

"Why were you drugging me?"

The image focused in her head. He'd had a needle going into the vein on her arm. Reflex made her clench the crook of her elbow with the opposite hand as if she could protect herself by doing so.

"I wasn't. I was saving your life!"

"Come again?"

He reached for her and placed his hands on her shoulders. She shrugged him off before he could put his palms fully onto the T-shirt.

"Don't touch me!"

He lifted his hands, palms out, in a gesture of surrender. "Please, sit down. There's so much you don't know."

"Then enlighten me."

He sighed. "Sit down. Please."

Her legs were starting to wobble under her. If it weren't for that, she would have stood her ground.

He returned to the coffee table, parking his arse on the edge of the solid wood as he bent forward, facing her. "I *was* giving you a drug, but it was an antidote to a neurotoxin Evangeline had placed inside your home so you'd go mad and die a slow death."

This sounded more and more like a twisted plot to assassinate an Eastern European world leader or something. Who was she to be implicated in such a complex scenario? She organized companies' events and sometimes made their ads, for goodness' sake.

"That's why you were getting forgetful, why you fell off the ladder. Evangeline had placed this proprietary compound over your head in the bedroom, inside your headboard ..."

What the fuck? Before he'd even stopped talking, she shot to her feet and careened down the side of the living room to the hallway leading to her bedroom. On the threshold, she paused. One glance at the torn headboard—the space where it had been now the naked grey concrete of the wall—and she lost it. She had just enough time to rush to the powder room at the end of the corridor and throw up in the sink.

Someone had tried to kill her.

And the fire? She ran the tap so she could rinse her mouth, then asked Zach the question as he joined her side.

He nodded, and she provided no resistance, defeated, as he pulled her into his arms to carry her to the sofa again.

"But ... why?" she railed. "Why me? Dax left me so long ago."

"He said two things before he died—"

"He's dead?" Shock froze her, but then, tears welled in her eyes. She didn't know where the certainty came from, but she spoke it out loud. "She killed him, didn't she?"

He simply nodded.

"How?"

"Bullet wound. It was a gun for hire."

Zach reached for her hands. Too stunned by all this information, she let him wrap his large palms around her cold fingers.

"Vosloo said two things before he died. One we figured to be your name. The other word? It doesn't make sense to us."

"And?"

"And we think you might know what it means."

At this point, she was so overwrought, she wouldn't have been able to fight even if she'd wanted to. "Go on."

"Viarbe. Does it mean anything to you?"

"I would bet that word doesn't exist in any language."

"So you don't know?"

Something in his tone rubbed her the wrong way, and she squinted, narrowing her gaze onto him. Zach knew all this; he was here for this very reason. Why? What did all this conceal?

"What's it to you?" she asked.

He cursed. "Damn it, Annabelle. Don't you see we have to find this killer—?"

"We?" she interrupted him, dislodging her hands from his grip and sending his arms flying. "I'm pretty sure this 'we' isn't referring to you and me. So who the hell is 'we', Zach? And come to think of it, how does Jonathan fit in? How is he your partner?"

"The damn blabbermouth—"

"Answer me!"

"It's complicated." He sighed and ran a hand over his shaved head.

"So un-complicate it."

"I am not at liberty to discuss any more with you."

She huffed. "It's classified?"

"Something like that."

He knew all this and more, and he was on the trail of a psycho killer. She bit her lip as the facts added up in her mind.

"Who are you really, Zach?"

He clenched his jaw and looked away.

"Are you the police? Interpol?"

He shook his head.

He wasn't Mauritian, yet, he was operating on Mauritian soil. The only people who would have such jurisdiction were ... She gulped as the idea hit.

"You're a spy?"

He didn't need to nod for her to know she'd hit bull's eye.

"What are you doing at my agency?" she continued. Might as well get as many answers as she could. "Is that a ... cover?"

"Yes. But the Wexler-Prinsloo deal is a real thing. I only rode in on the coattails of it."

So there was at least a silver lining to all this. Sparkle might indeed join the worldwide WP network, after all. If she didn't die first from exposure to some neurotoxin or fire catching around her pool.

"A cover for what?" she continued.

"Protecting you," he replied, still not looking her way.

She snorted. "Great job you've done of it so far."

He didn't say anything, just lowered his head. Something went off inside her overactive imagination;

she read way too much fiction to not think of all the avenues this scenario could've taken.

"Wait a second. You thought I was *her*?"

He still didn't look at her. "Everything pointed in that direction, yes. Whenever there's been an Evangeline kill abroad, you were also there with Dax."

True, the two of them *had* travelled a lot. Dax loved to up and run to some exotic destination at the drop of a hat. It had been a deal-breaker between them because he'd wanted to keep on with this kind of life while she'd wanted to settle down and have a family one day. Until Mr. Right would come along, she had resigned herself to slumming it with the Mr. Right Now Dax had been. He'd been fun, what could she say?

And to think it had all been a cover to help an assassin make her kills.

To imagine Zach had even thought her capable of something like that ... Fury stormed in to set fire to her blood.

"Get out," she said softly.

He finally turned to look at her. "Annabelle—"

"Leave. Piss off. Go away, Zach. If that is even your name."

"It *is* my name. I can assure you of it. You're still in danger."

"And I don't feel safe with you around. Tell that to your boss or whoever you report to."

A quick glance at the digital clock on the demi-console against the wall showed her it was close to six a.m. on Monday, February Nine. Drat. She would be late for work. The whole weekend had gone down the dumps with her getting nothing done except brush with death more than once. She had to get ready.

She glanced at her attire and shivered. These clothes were dirty and wrinkled. And her hair—she winced when she touched her locks. What the hell had they done to her tresses? She'd need at least one hour of leave-in conditioning mask in there for it to start looking healthy again. It was the price to pay when going for so many extensions. She'd always had thin, flat hair, though. This had been a price she'd paid willingly.

"Annabelle—"

"Get lost, Zach."

She got up to go to her bathroom before he said anything. Inside her bedroom, she forced herself not to look at the ripped headboard and quelled her nausea once again. Someone had tried to kill her by poisoning her then setting her house on fire. The bitch was bringing it on, and the only protection Annabelle had was the liar in her midst.

But rather than cower and wait for the killer to strike, she chose to go away dancing to her own tune. She would *not* stop living, never mind the target painted on her back. The people looking for the psycho must be cunning and resourceful—international agencies like the CIA, SIS, and Mossad always were. Whoever had sent Zach here should be able to do their job correctly and get this assassin apprehended.

Annabelle was *not* going to play the victim.

So with all guns blazing, she got ready and set out to go to the Sparkle office in the capital. Her moxie, however, took a blow when she found Zach sitting at the glass table in the veranda punching away at the keyboard of his laptop. The rat.

"What are you doing here?" she hissed, never mind how no one else was there yet to hear her.

"I told you the Wexler-Prinsloo deal was still on," he replied coolly.

She fumed. That meant he had her by the short and curlies. He was still the agency rep who would make or break their adhesion to the organization.

"Fine," she huffed as she turned on her heel. "Stay out of my way, and we'll be just fine."

Annabelle raged for the rest of the day because Zach didn't leave her side an inch when she had clearly told him to go get lost in some dark corner somewhere. She didn't need his protection.

When his Jaguar followed her small hatchback into her house's courtyard, and he came out and made to get into the house, she lost her shit.

Stalking after him because he'd gone ahead and entered the house already while she'd been silently seething on the porch, she pounded the marble flooring with her high heels as she went around her place looking for him. She finally found him in the hallway leading to the bedrooms. A glance inside the guest room and at the neatly arranged suitcases near the bed cut her vocal cords. But not for long.

"You moved in? I'm sorry, but I wasn't consulted or anything, given how it's my house and all!"

"You need protecting," he grumbled.

"Then protect me from afar. You don't need to be here—"

"Damn you, woman! Don't you know when to quit?"

Annabelle's mouth hung open. Seriously? The gall of the male chauvinist prick! She took in a deep breath to fuel her next tirade, but he beat her to the punch.

Zach turned on her, marching up to her and getting so close that he all but made her back slam into the smooth façade of the bedroom wall.

"I can't let you die, do you get it? Not on my watch, not ever. Do you know—" his voice had grown strangled. "Do you know what it did to me, to imagine you had died? To think for those never-ending seconds until I could get into the water and grab your lifeless body and pull you to me, to feel for your pulse, that it was too late? That *I* had been too late and had failed you?"

She swallowed hard as he got closer, unable to form a coherent thought in her mind.

His hand came up and clasped the side of her face. His palm unfurled over her jaw, the heat in his skin diffusing into her as the strength in his hand gave her an anchor in the storm that was her existence. She couldn't force a word across her lips as she took in what he'd said to her, the naked and unabashed hurting still echoing from them.

Zach then lowered his head and pressed his forehead to hers.

"Do you?" he asked softly.

Her lips parted, and she gulped back. She recalled what it felt like to be on the brink of death, to see her regrets flashing in front of her eyes and knowing she would never get to live to erase the remorse of things she hadn't done—things she'd been too chicken to do.

Yes, she knew what death's embrace felt like, and with it still looming above her like Damocles' sword, she couldn't but seize every moment of life she got to take.

She couldn't but seize *him* when he stood in front of her like this.

So paying heed only to the voice telling her to live for now and avoid regrets, she bridged the gap between Zach's lips and hers and kissed him.

An inferno not unlike the one that had blazed around her pool flared to life inside her, and she'd bet, in him, as well. Because her kiss seemed to have been the only cue he'd been waiting for.

Both his hands came up to clasp her face in his gentle but hot grip as he pressed his taut, muscular body into her and flattened her back against the wall. Her breasts got squashed against his hard chest, but what a delightful feeling this was, to be at his mercy and totally claimed by him like this.

His tongue parted her lips, and she tilted her head to the side to allow him in even more. He tasted of coffee and mint and a flavour that was all man and all Zach. She could get drunk on it if she let herself go.

The cold against her back provided a startling contrast against the heat of his body radiating onto her front, making her crave his warmth even more. Because even her soul had grown cold, not having known the touch of a man—let alone basked in his love—for so long. But all this was ending tonight. Because she had him now. Even if just for one encounter.

His hands left her jaw to roam down the column of her throat, his fingers threading a tingling path as they tickled softly over her collarbones. Her legs almost gave in under her, and he seemed so attuned with her, he brought his hands down to cup her arse and got her to lift her legs so she could wrap them around him. She did just that, relishing the feel of his solid obliques against her inner thighs, and then settled her legs against the thin cotton of his shirt. With her free hands, she slid the jacket off his shoulders and helped him shrug out of it.

Zach pushed her even further against the wall. The breath got knocked out of her—but was it from being slammed into the concrete or from his nose nuzzling in the valley between her breasts? Wow, she hadn't realized he'd lifted her up to the perfect level so he'd just have to tilt his head forward for his mouth to latch onto an exposed nipple after he'd pulled the bra cups down.

A rush of moisture coursed down her feminine core as he toyed with and rolled the pointed tip using his lips and tongue. When his teeth gently joined the fray, she whimpered, sure she had drenched the front of his trousers.

The rigid feel of his erection made itself known against her mound, and she squirmed.

"Now," she muttered as she let her head loll back against the wall while he'd switched to the other nipple.

He must've sensed her urgency, because his mouth let go, his fingers getting busy with the silky ties at her waist. He paused, and she looked down. Right. Why on Earth had she decided to wear a jumpsuit today? These were logistical nightmares to get around.

Unless the guy simply grabbed the two sides and ripped the thing open along its seam. Yeah, that would work well, too. She didn't even cringe at the sound the silk made as he tore the garment apart.

She felt him make quick work of his button and zipper, then, the thick, engorged head of his cock was pressing against her folds. Delightful shivers of pleasure were already coursing through her from imagining him taking her.

She closed her eyes and bit her lip strongly enough to draw blood when he surged into her and made her his.

Yes, this was what living felt like. *Take that, bitch,* she told Death inside her head.

Zach kept thrusting, caressing her throat with his lips, his breath warm and moist against the shell of her ear. Harder, faster, he took her. His mind-numbing rhythm called to her, urged her to keep up, to meet him stride for stride, pushing her and rushing her to a finish line waiting for her somewhere high above in the clouds.

Then, her world shattered in one moment. Her thoughts merged into a kaleidoscope of mumbo-jumbo nonsense as all the colours in the Universe converged onto her and exploded in the most blinding and pure white light she had ever encountered when her orgasm rocked through her.

She heard Zach's breathless gasps from afar.

"Annabelle," he breathed and came.

She had never heard her name sound so beautiful.

Time stopped as they came back from their high. Slowly, she started making out the sounds of their ragged breaths, the pounding of her heart, and the whoosh of blood at her temples, the stickiness of sweat where their skin was touching, the heat still blazing from their bodies.

Zach reached up with his hands and gently got her to lay her head on his shoulder. With her weight almost entirely lying on his torso, he settled his forearms under her thighs and held her tighter against him. He started moving, then, and a few paces later, her back was touching the downy duvet on her bed.

She opened her eyes to find him leaning over her, his face serious, eyes intense.

A shudder of apprehension laced with worry coursed through her. It was all fine and dandy to live for now during the rush of anticipation and sex, but afterwards, what happened?

She blinked and then bit the side of her lower lip, looking up at him with wide eyes.

"What now?" she asked, so softly, she wondered if she had even said the words.

He remained silent, and the chaste kiss he deposited on her forehead brought her no closer to an answer, either.

CHAPTER SEVEN

Curepipe, Mauritius.
Wednesday, February 11. 5.40 p.m.

Zach glanced around him, and his brows furrowed. The front salon and opened porch of yet another period dwelling this time farther inland on the island were packed to the gills. People milled about with flutes of pink champagne in their hands while waiters drifted around with plateaus of canapés and mini versions of the French pastries that had made the Avignon name worldwide.

His instincts rose on high alert. There were too many variables at play here that could put Annabelle in danger. Alexis had all but placed him into the role of her bodyguard, and with his damn mark intent on going along with her over-the-top social life as if a killer weren't waiting for her at the next turn, he had his work cut out for him. So he stuck close to her while Jonathan worked in the background with Corpus resources to pinpoint a pattern to Evangeline's madness and hopefully find her location before it was too late.

His hand itched to go to his side under his suit jacket, but the Heckler & Koch P30 wouldn't be there. Mauritius was very stringent on gun possession, and his concealed carry permit was moot here in the scheme of the legislation. Furthermore, as a NOC—an agent with no official cover from a covert agency like the CIA or SIS or even a government—he couldn't take the risk of carrying here and then being prosecuted for it. The Corpus would not swoop in to get him out of such quicksand.

It had been a while since he'd been on bodyguard duty, but he knew his job today was to protect his client and get her out of the danger zone should any trouble arise. In such tight quarters, too, with so many people around, pulling out a gun would prove more dangerous than anything, the risk of collateral damage too high.

So the semi-automatic weapon had stayed at the Balaclava home. He'd been slipping it back into his suitcase when Annabelle had stepped into the guest bedroom and seen him handling the armed weapon. She had blanched at the sight, had shaken her head and refused to talk to him all the way here.

He snorted. 'Friendly but not familiar' was the first rule bodyguards were supposed to follow with their clients. They'd had no trouble keeping to this part of the deal this afternoon.

But looking at her now, one wouldn't know how shook she had been at the house. She smiled and laughed as she worked the room with expert poise and confidence, the grace in her movement fluid and never over-emphasized as if she were putting on airs. Her team handled the details of the event as she mixed in with the guests all while keeping an eye on the proceedings.

Many in her professional position would've chosen something tailored and in dark colours or neutrals. Not Annabelle, though. She wore an off-the-shoulders lilac dress making her resemble a glamorous fifties movie starlet, the hem of the wavy skirt flirting with her knees, her feet encased in delicate silver sandals that looked like they'd break if she so much as lifted the foot too high.

She walked the room with purpose, though, a real namesake for her agency tonight. She positively sparkled—the tiny crystals on her dress catching the light also reflecting in the smooth and silky waves of her thick hair that bounced and danced around her rounded shoulders.

To anyone looking, she radiated. But he knew the truth. The twinkle was gone from those gunmetal grey eyes. Ever since the moment she'd woken up after her ordeal with the Varden antidote, her gaze had gone dull. It even seemed pained now whenever she looked at him.

"*What now?*" she had asked after the first time they'd joined their bodies into one and found the sort of communion people only dreamed of experiencing even just once in their lives.

He hadn't had an answer for her. He still didn't. The only thing he knew for sure—he had to protect her. Never mind that he had feelings for her, ones he didn't wish to look too much in the face, actually. She would get a chance to live, to do even greater things in her life.

He scanned the room again, then returned his gaze onto her. Annabelle was embracing an older White woman with the regal carriage of a European queen. The thirty-something blond man with her then reached for her with a broad smile and proceeded to clasp her shoulders and kiss her on both cheeks.

Zach didn't like the familiarity between them. No one had the right to touch her—

But you do?

The thought slammed into his mind to attack the jealousy flaring in him like water destroyed the integrity of tissue paper. True, he had no right, either. God knew he was fucking up his job and his life with this situation—the first rule was to never get attached. When this mission was over, he would have to leave, and she couldn't come with him.

She deserved so much better ... but a selfish part of him couldn't let her go so quickly. Yes, it would be the right thing to do. To stop being so familiar with her. To end gracing her bed after sticking by her side all day at the office.

They were both hiding their heads in the sand, though. Annabelle hadn't asked any question about the future after their first encounter. Guess she also had her reasons for wanting to stay in this bubble where, so far, Evangeline hadn't gotten to them again.

A tingling at the back of his neck had Zach's senses going on full alert. He zeroed his gaze on Annabelle. A tall brunette with tanned skin, a look screaming 'Italian bombshell' at first glance, had now approached her, and even from twenty feet away, he could feel the animosity and guardedness coming from the beautiful creature.

Could this be the woman they were looking for? She'd gotten close to Annabelle.

"Chill, Zach," Haseena said as she sidled up to him. "They always remain civil when they meet."

He blinked as he let his shoulders relax. So this wasn't a threat. He turned to Haseena, whose thumbs were flying over the keyboard of her Smartphone as she updated some social media feed or the other with images and captions from the launch.

He glanced back at Annabelle. The blond man had his arm casually slung around the brunette's waist, and she stood way too close to him for anyone to misread that he belonged to her.

He nodded towards them when Haseena looked up again. "What's the story there?"

"Oh, that. Juicy one. The older woman is Agnès Armont-Marivaux. Unofficially the social queen of Mauritius. They say nothing happens in 'good' society without her knowledge and say-so. She's not even Mauritian, by the way. French-born and raised, daughter of a *duc*, married the equivalent of local White nobility here."

The name was ringing a bell in his mind. Where had he come across it?

Haseena continued prattling. "The man with her is her son, Eric. Renowned paediatrician. She wanted him to marry Annabelle, and for some time, it really looked like these two were going to walk down the aisle. Then Lara happened. She's the woman with him. His wife."

Now, the name made sense. He'd read it in Annabelle's file. Nothing had mentioned they'd been engaged, though. Zach frowned as he watched Annabelle once the couple and the older woman had stepped away. Her face looked shuttered, the corners of her lips pinched and a tad too pale.

Seemed she was unlucky in love. If she hadn't had feelings for this Eric fellow, the presence of the man's wife wouldn't rattle her so much. Then Dax Vosloo had come in and done his nasty number on her.

And Zach? He was playing with her, too. What else could he call it? As crude as it sounded, he had no intention of sticking here once they'd found Evangeline. Alexis was bound to need him on another mission. What would he do without the Corpus? That's what he was, a field agent.

He should break it off with Annabelle, whatever this was between them. Neither of them had given it a name, even when they'd gazed into each other's eyes the previous night and had decided of a silent accord to get into the same bed.

Someone seemed to call her name, and she turned in that direction. Zach caught the split-second when she closed her eyes then popped them open before slipping on the bright smile on her face once more. She approached the man who had called out, and she laughed at something he said then took his elbow to direct him towards Agnès Armont-Marivaux, making the presentations between them.

He glanced around the room, seeing the smiles on everyone's faces, the joy in their eyes, their wonder over the food being served. The launch event was a smash hit. Annabelle was well on her way to cementing her position as a leader in the communications field locally.

Before the shit had hit the fan, when she'd simply thought him to be the Wexler-Prinsloo rep at the office, she'd told him what it meant for her to ace this launch. She might have international contracts—Sparkle and Glitter, the ads arm, were the ones who had come up with the already iconic campaign that had put Elriksen Shipping, a Swedish company, on the map.

Her concept had been of a split screen advert where one half had shown a package being entrusted to the maritime company for transport and the other showing a fussy baby being cared for and waited on hand and foot. Both had moade clever use of the same backdrop and a voice-over saying 'Elriksen Shipping. Because we care' at the end, clearly suggesting the way the baby was being treated was how any package Elriksen Shipping handled would also be dealt with. The campaign had won awards the world over. The second advert she'd made for them in the same vein had had a pack of rambunctious dogs on a leash instead of a baby on the right side of the screen.

Because of the recognition she had garnered, international companies reached out to her. But she hadn't yet made her mark in front of the local competition on the Mauritian market.

Launching Avignon with a bang would seal the top spot for her. And the smash was happening, right before his eyes. He was happy for her. Simon Wexler wouldn't be able to deny her a partnership with his agency, and she'd win there, too.

The thought jolted him.

Wexler-Prinsloo was a front for the Corpus. They moved operatives using the comms agency's many offices over the African continent, as well as information and resources along its network. Annabelle would be exposed to all of it, too, even though she wouldn't know it.

She'd be in danger.

The protective instinct inside him that didn't want to see her hurt was quick to tell him he should sabotage this partnership venture before it could come to fruition. She would be safe then.

But the other part of his gut, the one that had been honed from over a decade in the military and spy game, told him something else. How he should look at her really closely now and see what stern stuff she was made of. The woman had the shadow of probably the most dangerous assassin to exist floating menacingly over her, yet, look at her tonight. Composed, on top of her game.

Not scared at all. If she was, she sure knew how to hide it.

No, he should not dismiss her as weak and fragile. He'd watched her working the room tonight, being the social butterfly, yet having an iron grip on every aspect of this event even when she was in the spotlight and everything was happening backstage.

Annabelle de Castelban would make a fantastic agent of influence if the Corpus could get her in its ranks.

If they trained her, she would be safe. Never mind that he and she would work for the same agency. She would never leave Sparkle—it was her baby—and he didn't see what he would be doing on this tiny island once she'd been turned into at least an asset for Alexis.

Their paths *could* cross again … though they shouldn't. The two of them had no future together.

But he wouldn't leave her in the lurch. Not on his life. Did it, however, mean he could recruit her into the ranks he'd been serving since soon after he'd finished university?

His gut told him to do it. The same certainty that rang in his head when he just knew he had a perfect shot on a target was making itself heard right now, too.

So he pulled his phone out and sent an encrypted text to Alexis, telling her of his assessment as he watched Annabelle tonight. He then pocketed the device and returned his gaze to her. Until he got further directives, he would stay put and keep playing the part of her dutiful and ultra-aware bodyguard.

The ball was now in the boss' court.

***

Balaclava, Mauritius.
Wednesday, February 11. 11.24 p.m.

Annabelle hid a grimace as she entered her house and made a beeline for the sofa. As soon as she plopped down onto it, she lifted one foot, ditched the shoe on it, and did the same with the other one. Those slinky ties had started to eat into her skin at some point, but she'd borne the pain and had kept on smiling like a clown at a circus. Not anymore, though. Now, she was in the safety of her home.

Which has been breached by a psychopath assassin twice, a little voice whispered.

She snorted and dismissed the disturbing thought with an imaginary wave of her hand. Death in itself didn't scare her. Not living the life she had left, though—yeah, that made her shit her trousers.

"Why do women persist on wearing such instruments of torture?" Zach asked as he settled at the opposite end of the sofa, placing his discarded jacket over the arm.

She rolled her eyes at him. "You're a guy. You won't understand."

He chuckled. What a delightful sound. He should laugh more often. She would love to keep hearing that at least once a day.

She winced at the thought. She shouldn't be thinking of anything with him. Because Zach wasn't hers. He would never be. She might've had him in her bed for the past two nights, but it had been just an interlude in the big scheme of things. She'd watched enough James Bond movies to know how the hard-hearted spy's countenance melted just enough for him to spend some time with the damsel in distress, then it would grow to stone again, and duty would prevail, taking him away from her.

She bit her lip, tasting the sweet, raspberry flavour of the Dior lip tattoo tint she'd worn tonight to be sure her lip colour wouldn't fade throughout this evening.

What could she do except let him go? Men never stayed around for the long haul with her. The sooner she accepted it as her reality, the better, right?

The quiet inside the house felt too oppressive. She reached for her cell phone, which she had ditched on the coffee table, and started a relaxing playlist. The Bluetooth speakers around the room picked up on the signal, and a woman's voice stating she'd known the guy was trouble since he walked in made itself heard.

Across from her, Zach groaned.

"What?" she asked with a frown.

He shook his head. "Who is that?"

"Taylor Swift, duh."

"What is it with you and pop music?"

She raised her eyebrows.

"I didn't know I had a purist with me here." She then squinted at him. "Let me guess … Opera?"

She had gone with the opposite end of the spectrum.

He winced. "What's wrong with classical?"

"Oh, dear," she muttered, but laughed inside. It would be so fun to rile him. "Give it a chance."

"Trust me, I've been giving it a chance every time I get into your car."

"Those modern arias aren't going to kill you," she said as she brought her feet up onto the cushions and started to rub the sensitive soles now burning.

"Says you," he retorted as he lunged forward and grabbed her ankles, tugging her to him.

She squeaked, the sound turning into a moan of pleasure when he placed her feet on his lap and started using his thumbs to massage the soles. His strong fingers gripped the top of her feet in the perfect hold to ease the tension and pain in the tendons.

He kept on with the ministrations, and she quelled the sounds that made it seem like she was experiencing an orgasm directly through his foot rub.

The music changed, Nickelback's 'Satellite' now on. Listening to the opening lyrics brought a pang to her heart. She, too, had something on her mind, and it had also never been the right time to say it aloud, either. Recently, life had shown her just how easily it could slip past someone, and they could never get the time lost back.

Annabelle didn't know from where she grabbed on to the remnants of her courage as she stared him straight in the face.

"Zach, when all this is over, you're going to leave, aren't you?"

His face grew shuttered, jaw clamping. She thought he wouldn't answer until he nodded.

"Yes," he clipped out. "I'm sorry."

No need to be, she wanted to say, but couldn't. Instead, she tugged her feet from his grip, then put them down on the floor and stood.

Next, she extended a hand to him. "Dance with me, Zach. Like tonight's our only night."

In the background, Chad Kroeger's voice echoed those same last words in the song.

She waited with bated breath as Zach watched her with narrowed eyes then blinked as if coming to a decision. Getting up from the sofa, he took her extended hand in his and drew her to him.

At five-foot-nine, Annabelle had never considered herself a small woman by any standard. But barefoot in front of Zach's staggering six-foot-three, she felt tiny. When she went to him and his arms closed around her back, her cheek landed just perfectly in the hollow between his sculpted pecs.

"Gotta be careful not to step on any cat," he murmured in her ear.

She smiled against his shirt. He needn't worry—the cats were asleep in their beds at the side of the kitchen. He was only trampling her heart, but then again, she had willingly given it to him to trample on when she had asked him to dance with her.

The music wrapped around them, ensconcing them in a bubble. If she died like this, she'd die happy. But Jonathan was on the lookout outside, and the two men had placed paraphernalia of security devices like motion sensors all over the property. Evangeline wouldn't be able to catch them unawares.

So with the thought securely in her heart, Annabelle surrendered and let herself go against Zach's solid, warm body. He smelled a little of sweat, an aroma making him all man and absolutely irresistible.

Martin Garrix's 'So Far Away' came up next, and hearing those poignant lyrics about how the singer was looking for this person in the dark, asking her to show herself to him, tore her heart in two. Because that's what would happen to her once Zach stepped out of her life. He would be gone forever. She wouldn't know how to love someone else, either, just as she wouldn't know how to forget his face.

It didn't matter if they'd known each other only a few days. He'd left a mark on her, one she knew she couldn't ever erase.

A tear slipped from the corner of her eye, and she reached up and brushed it away.

The movement must've alerted Zach to her state of mind because he pulled away from her and gazed down into her face. She didn't hide the next tear. *Couldn't* hide it.

The two of them could've had the stars together if they'd been given a chance.

She saw the same certainty reflected in the tick of his clenched jaw, in the narrowing of his eyes where a flare of pain echoed the agony the same lance was piercing through her.

He felt it all, too. Knew it. If only things were different, their feelings allowed to grow and roam freely like a normal couple.

Normal. She wanted to laugh at the thought, but her chest squeezed at the notion. At the intense desire for this to be her reality.

Normal.

When he bowed his head forward and kissed her, she closed her eyes, and along with them, the shutters on anything that could have been between them. She went willingly when he bent and scooped her up with one arm under her knees.

He carried her into the bedroom and laid her on the bed. Lifting her shoulders off the mattress, she tightened her arms around his neck, holding him close to her, not allowing their kiss to break. When her legs came up and wrapped around his waist, he propped himself on his forearms and let some of his weight fall onto her.

Annabelle sighed against his mouth. How she loved this feeling of sinking into the bed under his body. Raw power pulsed along those strained, buff muscles, but she knew he would never hurt her. No, he just wrapped her in his strength, cocooned her in his embrace, and made her world shrink to this space where they existed together.

They kissed for a long time, then he trailed his mouth down her jaw, her neck, eliciting little gasping moans from the back of her throat. He kissed her body over the fabric of her dress, making her giggle, and when he reached the flowy skirt, he pushed the gauzy layers up until fresh air blowing in from the air-conditioning vents tickled the now-exposed skin of her limbs.

Slowly, gently, he removed her lacy knickers. She squirmed as he kissed his way up one inner thigh, the anticipation almost killing her, and she sucked in a breath and clasped the sheets in her tight grip when he settled his mouth on her core. Yes, they'd had sex two nights in a row, but it had been just mindless fucking. He hadn't kissed her there—they'd been too busy ditching the preliminaries to get right to the act that would make them come harder every single time.

They hadn't made love.

But tonight was different.

He kissed and fondled her, his tongue teasing her clit just slowly enough to drive her mad with wanting. The rascal—she could feel him smiling against her. A gasp tore out of her when he pushed two fingers inside her, and his lips settled on her clit to suckle it deep and hard.

Her back arched from the bed, her orgasm ripping through her without much more prompt because he had already taken her to the crest of the wave and she just had to let go to soar into its downward crash.

When she managed to come back to the surface again, it was to the feeling of Zach depositing soft kisses on her belly. He glanced up then, and their eyes met, speaking a language only two people who had found the full communion of their bodies and hearts could understand.

"Come here," she whispered as she opened her arms to him.

He complied without a word, and after he'd slid his body over hers, the fabric of his shirt catching at a few points on the crystals in her dress, she clasped his strong jaw in both her palms and lifted her head to kiss him.

She tasted herself on his lips. A bit kinky, but she relished the sensation because she was getting to share this moment with him. And speaking of that, she hadn't tasted him yet. She'd asked him to treat this night as if it were their last—she shouldn't lose out on this opportunity, either.

So Annabelle rolled her body over and pushed him along until he lay flat on his back on the mattress. They kissed again, then she returned the same favour he'd bestowed upon her. Her lips travelled over his chin and jaw, the close-cut goatee scratching the sensitive skin of her face. But it was a pleasant burn, all things considered. As she continued her trek down, his skin tasted salty and reeked of a soft musk that was masculine and all Zach. He didn't seem to wear cologne. All the better. She loved his scent and would bottle it up and inhale it like a fix every day if she could.

She trailed kisses over his brushed cotton shirt, and once at his trousers, she paused to undo the belt then the button and zipper. His engorged erection sprang free; she giggled when she realized he had gone commando under the suit.

She stopped for a moment to drink her fill of the sight of him. He was beautiful everywhere, his skin a golden, hairless, and smooth amber glowing in the muted light of the sconces on the wall.

His proud cock had also gotten the memo stating he was a gorgeous male specimen. He was thick and long, perfectly proportioned, and the bead of glistening pre-cum forming at the tip of the bulbous head made her wet her lips in anticipation.

She wrapped her hand around the base of his shaft, surprised to find her thumb and middle finger couldn't meet across the girth. As she was lowering her head to take him into her mouth, he lifted his upper body, propped himself on his forearms as his sultry, intense eyes locked on her.

A challenge? He wanted to watch, eh. The pervert, she silently chided in her mind with an internal giggle. She loved when stakes were raised like that.

She lifted an eyebrow, then, holding his gaze, she parted her lips and slid them over the tip of his cock. He tasted salty and fresh, and she relished the flavour on her taste buds. When she added a flick of her tongue to the veiny underside, he closed his eyes, and a hiss escaped his lips. She smiled, jubilation singing inside her as she intensified the pressure of both her hand and her tongue. Dipping her mouth lower and lower, she took him in as deep as her throat would allow, then pulled away to start the torture all over again.

At one point, his body tensed. He wrapped his hand in her hair and pulled her off him, his cock falling out of her mouth with a soft 'pop.'

"I will blow in your mouth if you continue," he muttered as if out of breath.

She frowned. And what was wrong with that? It was nice he'd thought to warn her before, but it was exactly what she'd been going for. She made to lower her head again, but he stopped her, his grip still in her hair.

"Not like that," he said softly.

Not on our perfect night—she understood those unspoken words.

So she released him and got up on her knees to slide her body forward on the bed until she hovered just on top of him. Locking eyes with him, she pressed her hands flat on his chest then lowered herself, taking him inside her in the process.

They didn't break eye contact as she rode him. It was slow and sweet, hot and sensual, frenetic and passionate all into one.

At one point, Zach lifted himself up until he was almost sitting. His hand found its way into her hair once again, and with his grip on the back of her skull, he pulled her face to him so he could kiss her while surging his hips with more power against her. That sent her splintering into a shattering climax.

He drank the scream from her mouth, and she returned the favour moments later when he reached completion, too.

They tore apart then, out of breath, panting and huffing from the exhilarating rush they'd been on. Foreheads pressed, she kept her eyes closed, not wanting the moment to end. She'd say the same feeling was coursing through him, because he relinquished his grip on her head only just, his fingers twirling slowly in her locks before he closed his fist and tugged her head back. In doing so, he exposed her neck, and she moaned when he placed his hot mouth against the column of her throat and suckled the skin.

She giggled. "You'll give me a love bite."

He rumbled something unintelligible even while he didn't stop his assault.

When he pulled away, she didn't need to reach up and touch the spot to know he had left his mark on her. Her skin was smarting with a delicious pulsing at that point.

He released his grip on her hair and let his body fall back onto the mattress. Annabelle thought of following him and lying down on his body, but a thought made her stop. The adrenalin was coming down—he would feel the prick of the many crystals on her dress if she did this.

So she lifted herself off him and sidestepped over his body to get off the bed. The full-length mirror in the bathroom was clearly visible through the opened door, and she saw a woman with mussed hair and a slightly wrinkled dress standing, the parts of the man behind her on the bed visible in the reflection also showing clothes on him.

She shook her head. "We should stop meeting like that."

He frowned as he turned onto his side and in her direction. "Like what?"

She rolled her eyes as she turned to face him. "Like this. Having sex while we still have almost all our clothes on us."

And no protection on. She was covered with the pill, though, and he had told her he was safe after their first time.

He started smiling, and at the sight, lightness engulfed her whole being. Yes, they had no tomorrow, but they had now, and now was the stuff timeless memories were made of.

A phone vibrated somewhere. She narrowed her eyes as he reached into the pocket of his trousers and retrieved a cell phone. His brows furrowed as he read the text or the notification of whatever alert had just come in.

A shiver coursed down her back. Could it be Evangeline? Had the killer come for them?

"Is it …"

He glanced up then. "No."

Relief almost sapped the strength from her legs. But she shouldn't have rejoiced so quickly—a pall of dread fell over her as he sat up straighter, put the phone on the bedside table, then did the zipper and button on his trousers before looking up at her.

"Annabelle, we need to talk."

CHAPTER EIGHT

Balaclava, Mauritius.
Thursday, February 12. 1.30 a.m.

"Not now, Zach."

As he watched her whole countenance grow cold and shut down, Zach knew he was losing her. Something had happened, like a thread breaking or something. A line had been crossed.

She turned her back on him and went into the bathroom. Thankfully, she didn't slam the door closed behind her. He still had hope.

He got up from the bed, approached the threshold to find her pulling a wet wipe from a box and using it to cleanse herself. Next, she opened a drawer, pulled some knickers out, and then slipped them on.

Their night was over—she was making it clear. But he was the one who had stated the loaded words. They did need to talk. The message he'd just received was from Alexis, giving him the green light to tell Annabelle about the Corpus to gauge her reaction to their ideology before they could decide if she'd be willing to come on board.

She leaned forward in front of the mirror, and he winced when she peeled the fake eyelashes from her eyes.

"Annabelle—"

"Go away, Zach. I need to get this makeup off. It's late."

He sighed. "There'll be time enough for that later."

The glare she skewered him with would've had a less trained man scampering for cover.

"Please," he asked.

She rolled her eyes and closed the lid on the pot of solid cleansing oil on the counter. "Fine."

"Come here," he said.

"Why?"

"Because you'll freeze your feet off on the cold marble."

She muttered something under her breath and came back into the room. Bypassing the bed, she went to the high-backed sofa in the corner. Zach followed her and settled in the neighbouring seat.

He needed to tell her about the agency, sure, but in the past few minutes, ever since the fulminating orgasm that had ripped his every defence apart while he'd held her close to his body, tight in the lock of his arms, something had changed. He didn't want Annabelle to think him a cad who just swooped in, slept with a woman, and then drifted off when he'd finished his mission.

Oh, he knew why he needed her to have a better opinion and memory of him, and right then, he faced it. Because he had grown attached to her. Because she had impressed him with her beautiful and precious soul and had wheedled her way under his skin.

Because he had fallen in love with her.

She brought her feet up, knees almost touching her chin as she wrapped her arms around them. "You wanted to talk. So talk."

His breath hitched. Where did he start? He leaned forward and placed his forearms on his thighs.

"I was born in Tanzania."

"You told me. Your mother died when you were young, and you have a sister."

He nodded. "Her name is Zenobia. Our mother died when I was six, and she was three. Our father is an industrialist, lots of assets and stakes in mining and quarrying, as well as construction. He's a tycoon. Rich, busy." He paused as the grimace made its appearance on his face. "He didn't have time for two little kids. Less than a year later, he had remarried and had a new-born son. His wife, well, she didn't like us. Did I tell you she was a pale-skinned Ismaili like him? We were the dirty offspring she couldn't stand, more so Zenobia as my sister grew up into a woman so much more beautiful than she was. I was a boy, I could fend for myself. My sister couldn't."

"You protected her," Annabelle said softly.

He nodded. "I did. I even opted to go to university in Dar es Salaam and stay home so I could be with her. By the time I finished my MBA, she was on her way to medical school in London. My father wanted me to join the family business, but with Zayn safe, all I wanted was to get away from there. I never wanted to see him or that witch's face ever again. Our brother, Rayan ... well, he's not a bad kid. Misguided by his mother, sure, but we're civil."

He paused for a moment.

"I wanted to hit my father where it would hurt, let him know without a doubt how much I wanted to be away from him and his precious family. So I joined the Tanzania People's Defence Force, which made him livid. My superiors said I was good at being a soldier, and I was soon taking part in United Nations Peacekeeping missions. We were in Darfur, before the peace agreement, doing our darned best to help, but failing miserably. That's where I was recruited."

He looked up, and as he'd expected, he found confusion on her face.

Zach took a deep breath. "Into the ranks of the clandestine agency I still work for."

She frowned. "You mean, like the CIA or KGB or something?"

"It's the SVR now, not the KGB."

"Same difference. So?"

He shook his head. "Not exactly. The CIA, SVR, British SIS—they're covert. You know they're there, right, even if you don't know what they do. Clandestine means no one even knows the agency exists. Have you heard of the Corpus?"

"What?"

"Exactly. It's their name."

"And what do they do? Black ops or something?"

He chuckled.

"I mean, look at you," Annabelle continued. "On the trail of an assassin."

How would he explain it to her? Maybe the words of his mentor—who, at the time, he hadn't known had in fact been Tobias Friedrich in disguise—could shed some light for her.

"It's not black ops. At least, not like in the movies and TV shows. You know how the United Nations pass resolutions?" He waited for her to nod. "Well, resolutions are merely suggestions of good conduct. Countries don't always adhere to them. That's when you need a stealthy left hand operating clandestinely to do the job for you."

"Like apprehending international assassins?" she asked with raised eyebrows.

"Among other things. It's all about ideology. Meaning in the service of power. Actually being able to do something concrete."

"You help countries without boasting about it."

He smiled. "Exactly."

"But you don't kill people?"

He sighed. "Usually, no."

She raised her eyebrows as if asking for clarification.

Here comes the crash course into Corpus logistics.

"There are agents of influence, the ones who simply gather and drop information here and there and nudge things along the way. Then there are agent provocateurs, one step above, whose nudging gets much more hands-on. Both have licences to kill, but since every one of Corpus' missions is completely off any books, well, you try not to have any kills involved. That's what I am, by the way, depending on the requirements of the mission."

He paused for a breath. "Then there's the Kali. The bringer of death, the harbinger of destruction. She is an outright assassin, her targets being criminals that governments, international law enforcement, and covert agencies couldn't get to. Her job is to infiltrate the criminal's entourage, figure out how to bring down the entire organisation, then do just that as she also despatches the criminal to kingdom come."

Annabelle seemed stricken. "You know such women?"

He did, actually. The woman now at the head of aid agency Angelos was a former Kali.

"The Kali is lethal, Annabelle. She knows of a hundred and one ways to kill someone using poison alone and never leaving a trace so she can't get caught."

She blinked as she stared at him, mouth hanging open. "Are you saying Evangeline is a Kali?"

He nodded. "A little while ago, there was a mutiny inside the ranks of the agency. The leader was killed by a rogue faction wanting to cleanse the organization of those loyal to him and start their reign. Evangeline was their Kali, but she was, in short, just a twisted assassin since she had no ideology."

"Meaning in the service of power, right?"

"Yes. She served just her own psychopathic bents, answering to a woman who wanted to turn the Corpus into a bunch of mercenaries working for the highest bidder."

"What happened, with the mutiny?"

"It was quelled before it could make the ranks implode. The leader had unfortunately been murdered, but his daughter took over the agency, and she found out the mutiny had been the work of her own mother she'd thought dead all along."

He paused and sighed. He should tell her where he was coming from, what drove him to work for Corpus.

"Evangeline is the last trace of the mutiny the agency has yet to clean. The leader they killed? He was the man who recruited me, who saw something in me and offered me a job with his organization."

"He gave you purpose when you'd simply been intent on hurting your father."

Zach frowned. How did she know?

She shrugged. "We're all looking for meaning in our lives, Zach. A purpose and a path to wake up and see every day."

Seemed she had nailed it already. He hadn't figured this out until the head of the Corpus had become his mentor and taught him everything he knew. He'd vowed to help Alexis in any way he could to avenge her father's murder. Evangeline was the last thread they had to take care of. He wouldn't rest until she had been dealt with. Even though he'd fallen in love with a woman, who was as beautiful inside as she was outside. A woman who showed him, on nights like tonight, what life could be like for an average guy.

"So where do you work, usually?" she asked.

He could fib, but he didn't want to. "I'm based in Djibouti."

Her gaze narrowed. "Where they speak mainly French and Arabic. You understood French all along."

"I'm sorry."

He'd expected her to lash out, go into a wild rage. The Annabelle he had met last week had been that kind of impulsive and passionate woman who let her emotions power her. But then again, she had changed since the two assassination attempts on her.

How could he tell her how sorry he really was about all this? If he and the rest of the Corpus had been doing their jobs properly, they would've been able to apprehend the sadistic killer already, and Annabelle would've been safe.

Not so sure, a little voice chimed in. If they'd gotten to Evangeline after she had placed the Varden in Annabelle's bedroom, no one would've known she was being exposed to a deadly neurotoxin.

No one would've been able to save her life, then.

"You said you're *based* in Djibouti. That must mean you also work in other countries?" she asked.

A deflection from those dark thoughts. He'd take it. "Wherever the mission takes me."

"Like here."

He nodded.

She smiled. "Got a woman in every port, then?"

The blow hit hard, and he bent onto himself a bit more. "I wouldn't do that to you."

True, he had never let something serious develop between him and any woman he'd gotten involved with. He also wasn't a two-timing bastard.

"You know, with my luck, it wouldn't come as a surprise," she added.

Her luck in love. He remembered what Haseena had told him back at the launch, and curiosity, as well as red-hot jealousy, raged in him once more.

"What happened between you and that Eric guy?"

She raised an eyebrow. "You saw Lara approach me like she wants to go into an MMA ring with me, I suppose. Who filled you in? Daniel?"

He grimaced. It had, indeed, been the way the other woman had looked at her.

"Haseena," he replied.

"Of course." She laughed without mirth. "Agnès, Eric's mother, thought it was time for her only son to settle down a little while ago. At her daughter's engagement dinner, she invited every eligible young woman of 'good' French-Mauritian society to parade them in front of him. I was there, Eric singled me out, and he'd been fed up with her attempts at matchmaking, so when we saw we had her blessing, we decided to give it a try. I mean, he was nice and easy on the eyes, a paediatrician, and he was looking past my so-called society failings, so I thought we could make it work."

Zach frowned. So-called failings? She had none.

"Then what happened?" he asked.

"Then Lara happened." She gave a wistful smile. "Eric had been in love with her since their high school days. She had married someone else, though, but had just come back to Mauritius freshly divorced."

He frowned. "High school? She's from here? She's not Italian?"

Annabelle shook her head. "Lots of people think so, especially with her name. No, Lara is Mauritian, of Indian heritage. It was obvious he would've been miserable with me when he still carried a torch for her.

So I removed myself from the picture and let them pick up where they had left off."

"His wife doesn't know it?"

She shrugged. "I suppose she does. But it seems I have a reputation as a man-eater in their circles, and I guess she still thinks I might decide to come for her man should the urge tickle me someday."

She said all that as if she were talking of someone else, not like it was herself she was bringing down.

Zach stifled a curse, suddenly angry. "What's all this nonsense about you having failings and being a man-eater?"

She laughed, still without joy. "I was your mark, Zach. You should know all this about me."

The intensity of those gunmetal grey eyes on him made him squirm. She thought so little of him … and with good reason, too.

"Anyway, long story short, I studied post-grad in London after doing my degree at Paris Sorbonne. Got tangled there with a renowned British playboy by the name of Magnus Trammell. The party animal tag from my days with him never really left me."

She'd left unsaid how 'party animal' also came with 'slut' in a woman's case.

"I could've stayed there if I'd wanted to, with as clean a slate as I could get," she continued.

"What made you come back?"

She shrugged. "This is home. I missed the sun, the sea, how blue the African sky gets in winter."

He nodded. It was his case, too. He couldn't stand the greyness and dullness of places like Berlin and London when he knew of the vibrancy of the African continent. This land called to his blood.

"So you two broke up, and you came back here. It didn't end well between you?" he asked.

"Oh, we're still great friends. It just—" she shrugged. "—never ends up working out for me."

The smile she now gave him was genuine but sad. His heart squeezed in his chest. If he could do anything to make her life better, he would.

Getting her the Wexler-Prinsloo partnership might help. He would leave and go play espionage games on the African continent. She'd remain here, but with so much more great stuff to come if she landed this deal.

"Vosloo and you …" he started.

"A one-night stand that just wouldn't quit. He was a nice guy, you know. Funny, irreverent, bordering on silly, too, sometimes. In a way, he reminded me a lot of Magnus."

Zach winced. He did *not* want to hear about her being with other men and listen to the sweet feelings she'd had for them. Would she one day speak of him this way with a lover? His fist clenched as if with a mind of its own.

But she was paying him no heed, seemingly lost in her memories. Her arms had loosened their hold around her bent knees, and she was now playing with the sparkly trim on the hem of her dress.

"Dax and I had some good times. I still remember trying to teach him French. He was hopeless. He had this little pun he loved to use when he would go out every Sunday to go golf at the Gymkhana Club in Vacoas. He used to say 'Vilarbre' whenever he went there …"

Zach sat up straighter as the strange sound registered in his mind. "What did you just say?"

She blinked up at him as if coming out of a spell. "Hmm?"

"That word you just said. The one Vosloo used."

She frowned. "Vilarbre?"

His jaw dropped open, and he ran a hand over his face. "That's it."

"That's what?" she asked as she peered at him like he'd gone crazy.

"Before he died, Vosloo said two things. One was 'Annabwe,' which we figured was your name. The other word was 'viarbe.' It didn't make sense to us, but he knew you'd know. It must be this 'vilarbre' thing. What does it mean, Annabelle?"

She shook her head. "Zach, you're not making much sense here."

He left his seat to go crouch in front of her. Her eyes grew wide as he settled on his knees and reached out to clasp her hands in his.

"This has something to do with Evangeline, don't you see? Vosloo must've left some information with you, or something only you would know about. It's also why she is after you because she knows whatever you have will be damning for her."

She gently pulled her hands from his grip. "I know nothing of all this, Zach."

"No, you do," he maintained as he jumped to his feet and tugged her upright, too. "What does 'Vilarbre' mean?"

She waved a hand in the air. "It's a silly pun."

"About what?"

She gave an exasperated sigh. "Fine, have it your way. So Dax didn't know French, remember? Vilarbre is how he would butcher two words put together. *Ville* and *Arbre*, which mean—"

"Town and tree, respectively."

She glared at him. "Right, you know French. So the only town with a tree name in Mauritius is Vacoas. That's where he used to go golfing."

"Is it far from here?"

"A little less than an hour by car, if the traffic is fluid."

They wouldn't have less traffic than during night time. He grabbed her wrist and started towards the door. "Let's go."

She tugged her hand free and stood her ground. "Go where?"

He turned to face her. Couldn't she see she was making them lose time? "To this Vacoas place."

*

Annabelle stared at him agog. Seriously? He wanted them to go there now?

She threw a look at the clock in the hallway. "Zach, it's two in the morning."

"Precisely. We can go in and take a look and find whatever he's left for you and come back before anyone's the wiser. This won't be possible during the daytime when we don't have the cover of darkness."

Did he really hear himself talk?

"Are you out of your mind or what? I don't even have the slightest clue what you're looking for!"

"You'll know it when you see it."

Really? She raised her eyebrows and crossed her arms in front of her.

He sighed and looked up to the Heavens as if asking for patience. Wow. They must be overworking him at this Corpus agency or whatever.

"You said he used to golf there," he stated.

She shrugged. "At the Gymkhana Club, yes."

"Was there any place else in the town where he'd hang out?"

"Not that I know of. He was usually in there in the parking lot, out to golf, then he'd get back into his car and to his house on the West coast, in Rivière Noire."

"So the golf course premises are our best bet."

She sighed and watched him while she bit the inside of her cheek to stop herself from screaming. "Best bet for what?"

"To find what he left for you and only you to find."

"Zach, it's the middle of the night. Won't there, like, be security on the grounds or something?"

"Leave that to me."

Of course. Mr. Super Spy had this in hand. And try as she might to resist, she just knew he also wouldn't let up. It would be most comfortable to go along and prove him wrong as to this wild goose chase. The sooner she showed him all this, the sooner she could grab a few hours' sleep before she had to attend to another day at the office.

"Fine," she mumbled. "Let me get some shoes on."

At the cupboard by the front door, she pulled the panel open and raked her gaze over the shoes available. Her soles were still killing her from having been in those flimsy stilettos all night—heels were out of the question. Her attention landed on a pair of walking shoes, and she slid her feet into them without thinking twice. In her sparkly dress, she looked like a teenage-wannabe with the glittery trainers on her feet. At least no one would be seeing them in the dead of night.

She followed Zach with leaden limbs as he all but hopped along to his Jaguar F-Pace rental. When he entered the location into the GPS, she didn't even bother to correct him and let him know the system was giving them the most-travelled but also the longest route to get to Vacoas, by going through the capital city, Port-Louis, along the M2 motorway. She just didn't have it in her to give him directions to the alternate route on the Terre Rouge-Verdun Link

Road. Then, she frowned. Come to think of it, that road going up through a mountain range would be closed at this time, too. Just as well.

So she settled back and let him drive. He kept asking her to corroborate this whole *Vilarbre* thing—it was getting tedious, and she slammed the door open the second he stopped on the outskirts of the club on the main road bordering the golf course.

Once outside, the nippy cold of the air inland and on the upper plateaus where Vacoas was located assailed her and drove Goosebumps all over the naked skin of her arms and legs.

"Think, Annabelle," Zach kept going on as he stopped by her side. "Did he ever mention somewhere special here? Did you come here with him, and if yes, where did you go?"

She shook her head to try to clear the absurdity of this whole situation from her countenance. Maybe focusing on what he was asking would help.

Annabelle paused and thought back to the weeks spent with Dax. The only time she had come here with him had been when they'd met some of his friends. The men had played golf while she and the other guy's wife had strolled around in their wake—they had discussed the line of plastic-free shampoo bars and cosmetics she wanted to launch. Annabelle had gladly provided her with marketing tips and information about the local scene. Nothing had come from it, though. She'd heard soon after the woman had gotten pregnant with twins; she'd probably put her dream on the backburner.

After lunch that day, Dax had pulled her to him and kissed her soundly on the green, asking her if she wanted them to go steady from there on. They'd never spoken of it before then, but both had known there had never been any kind of commitment to their relationship so far. She'd said okay, and he had walked back with her, hand in hand, to the restaurant and bar.

A week later, he had left without a word.

She blinked as she thought of then, when she had, for one second, thought things might start looking brighter for her. Dax had been a forty-year-old South African expat who had sold a gaming app that had gone viral to some tech giant in Singapore. He wouldn't have needed to work another day of his life given the slam-dunk deal he'd made through the sale.

She frowned as something registered in her perception. On that day here, he had also done something she'd thought stupid but inherently endearing. Along the way back in after dropping his friends off in their car, he had made them stop at a tree where he had carved their initials inside a heart. It had been the first time someone had done this for her, and she had laughed at first, then she remembered running her hand over the gashes on the wood and asking the tree to forgive them for having hurt it this way. Dax had thought it silly, but she had known in her heart she had to do it.

She turned to Zach. "Wait, I think there might be something."

"What did you recall?" he asked as he clasped her elbow, his eyes dark and intense.

She blinked to break herself from the spell of his gaze and waved a hand in the direction of the road leading to the club. "Over there. There's a tree."

"Let's go."

He all but marched her along to the copse of tall, spindly trees growing on a piece of land resembling a triangle, with asphalted roads running on all three sides. She went along, and once on the site, oriented herself towards the entrance of the country club, after which she marched to the second to last tree on that edge.

"Do you have a light?" she asked Zach.

He turned on the flashlight on his phone and directed the beam onto the tree.

Annabelle gasped when the light hit the wood. She had almost expected the heart with D+A carved inside it to have faded away, or even for the tree to have been felled by Nature or Man. But no, there it was, in less stark glory than on the day she had last seen it, but there nevertheless.

"So this is it?" Zach asked.

She nodded.

"And?"

How would she know? He was the spy. So she simply shrugged.

He didn't say anything, just focused on the carving.

"Wait," he said. "What's that?"

"Where?"

"There." He pointed towards a series of little dots carved into the wood.

It looked like two parallel columns, two dots on the left, three on the right.

She frowned as she stared at it. "Does it even mean something?"

He snapped a picture after zooming in on the dots, then tapped onto the phone, probably sending it off to whatever brain worked with him in his clandestine agency.

"We'll know soon," he said as he looked up at her.

She'd swear it didn't take one minute for the phone to vibrate again. She'd hardly had time to adjust to the chill in the air at this late hour of the night.

"It's Braille," Zach said as he read the message.

"Braille? Dax had twenty/twenty eyesight."

"Maybe," he replied. "But did you know this system of dots can also be used as a last-resort code to impart information without arousing suspicions?"

Her eyes went wide, and she gasped. "Is that what this is? What does it say?"

"Below."

She glanced at the foot of the tree, just as Zach did. Before she could figure out what he intended to do, he had crouched down and was using his hands to dig out the grass at the base.

"What the hell are you doing?" she asked.

"Think, Annabelle. If he has hidden something below, and the heart and dots are a guide— wait. There!"

He raised his hand, brandishing a small re-sealable plastic bag. The clear surface was marred by dark earth, but she could make out the shape of something metallic in there. She squinted.

"Is that ..." she started.

"A USB key? Yes." Zach shot to his feet and clasped her elbow, marching her back to his SUV while she was still processing all this espionage craft.

"I need to check this as soon as possible," he said, and lobbed her the key fob for the Jag.

Oh, so she was on driving duty now, wasn't she? He didn't bother with her any more, just went to the back seat, retrieved the sleek laptop she had seen him use at Sparkle's office, and settled into the passenger seat with the computer open on his thighs.

She had been effectively dismissed. Shaking her head, she climbed into the driver's seat, closed the door, and pulled on her seatbelt. She cursed as she glanced around. No clutch pedal, and an automatic gearbox. Couldn't he have gone for a manual box like every sane person on the island? They said it was easier to drive an automatic. She'd never agreed, trusting the reliable clutch pedal to help her gauge her driving.

Still, she managed to get the vehicle started and have them on the road without crashing into a nearby tree. The brake pedal had less touch-happy responsiveness than her Picanto's, and she almost crossed a few lines at traffic lights because she hadn't braked enough to stop in time.

Zach all but ignored her as he furiously pounded at the keyboard. He must be in connection with someone—she could see his phone all lit-up and providing a Wi-Fi hotspot where he had slid it into the cup holder behind the gearbox.

"Damn it!" he cursed, and thumped the dashboard hard enough to make her jump in her seat.

"What is it?" she asked, her curiosity piqued.

"The bloody thing is encrypted! It will take at least twelve hours for the IT geniuses to crack it and find out what intel Vosloo has put on this stick. I thought getting past the password protection and the firewalls on the blasted thing would be enough to get us in." He cursed again, in a language she didn't know.

Based on his being from Tanzania, she would bet it was Swahili. It sounded something like *'fala.'*

They had reached her house, and after she stopped the Jag to input the code at the gate since she didn't have the fob with her, a wave of fatigue and weariness crashed over her. She brought the vehicle to a stop inside the courtyard.

"Now we can do nothing else but sit on our arses for twelve more fucking hours!" he went on as he exited the SUV and slammed the door with so much force that she flinched.

Fury rose inside her at his total lack of consideration for her in this whole episode. So they'd have to sit on their buttocks? Seemed to her they hadn't been doing anything else for the past week. Twelve more hours wouldn't hurt, would it?

"You're unbelievable," she muttered as she brushed past him towards the front door.

He grabbed her arm and made her stop. "What does that mean?"

She shrugged his grip off her with more force than necessary. His eyes narrowed under the gesture. She braced her shoulders and straightened her spine as she tilted her head back to look him in his now-menacing gaze.

"Well, how about, 'Thank you, Annabelle, for bringing me to the spot where I managed to find all the information I need about a killer I've been chasing for months without any luck until you stepped in'?"

Low blow, she knew, but she was done with being the nice girl in the whole deal. The nice girl always got fucked over.

"Or how about, 'Thanks, Annabelle, for coming with me in the dead of night on a wild goose chase when I know you had a tough day and evening and you will hardly get a couple hours' sleep now before you have to go back to the office'?"

"Thank you," he bit out.

She rolled her eyes at him. "You could at least say it as if you meant it."

"Look here—" he started.

"No, *you* look, Zach." She crossed her arms in front of her chest and jutted her chin out with determination. "I asked for none of this. I never thought my life would suddenly resemble some plot from *Mission: Impossible* or something. All things considered, I shouldn't be surprised if you just pulled your face off right now in front of me."

She really was losing her shit now—she reckoned it. But see if she cared. She was overwrought, tired, in need of sleep, with a face full of makeup and now starting to feel like thick goop on her skin, and she'd just been royally fucked by this man standing in front of her. Yes, literally and figuratively, because she'd been nothing but a pawn he'd been playing on this mission of his.

There, she stared reality in the face. It had never been about feelings or anything else. She'd been part of a job, full stop.

It hurt.

She turned and started towards the front door. The alarm would go off if she didn't input the code within a minute. She was doing just that when Zach stormed in behind her.

"What the hell are you talking about?" he asked.

She didn't answer. She'd had it up to here with this guy. He'd found what he'd come to Mauritius looking for—Dax's cryptic 'viarbe' statement. He should piss off now.

"Why would I pull my face off?" he continued.

She shook her head. "Don't you watch any espionage stuff? Ethan Hunt, *Mission: Impossible*? The spy who can turn into anyone by putting on a mask?"

He mumbled something in return. She didn't pause to listen, just went inside.

"Zach, I'm tired—"

The words died on her lips, and she froze on the edge of the living room. Zach almost bumped into her, and as he, too, registered the sight in front of them, his hands came up and clasped her shoulders hard.

There, on the sofa, sat a young, blonde woman, and she had a gun in her hand.

"Finally!" she exclaimed in a sweet, tiny voice more suited to a bubbly six-year-old. "I was wondering how much longer you would make me wait! The company is not fab here, I'll admit."

She pouted as she nodded towards the cats.

Oh, no, her babies! Had she hurt them? Annabelle risked a glance at the cat beds on the side. Riri and Fifi were on a cushion, and Loulou crouched low in front of them on the floor, his tail and the fur on his spine all spiky. When the woman so much as moved her hand in their direction, the tabby hissed at her.

He was protecting the other two. Dear, dear Loulou.

She returned her gaze to the woman. Somehow, she seemed familiar.

The blonde stood then, the gun still aimed at them.

"Evangeline," Zach said softly behind Annabelle.

Her heart rate skipped a beat in its rapid tattoo as he brought confirmation to her suspicions.

So this was the psycho assassin who had already tried to kill her twice.

Annabelle hadn't expected her to look like an airhead cheerleader.

"How did you get in?" he asked.

She reached into a pocket and removed a few little blue balls she let fall onto the floor. "Your motion sensors were way too obvious. As was the thermal detection unit near the wall. Corpus tech just isn't what it used to be, is it? The alarm was also a joke to bypass."

Zach tensed behind Annabelle.

"Let her go," he said. "Your beef is with the Corpus. Not with her."

Evangeline tutted. "Come on. You won't deny me a bit of fun, would you?"

Again with the pout. Did she think it actually worked? It looked downright creepy, like the Chucky doll or something.

"No, Lover Boy," she continued as she came towards them with the gun still aimed their way. "It all started with her. It all ends with her. Now be a good lad and step away, will you?"

A shiver of cold dread raced down Annabelle's spine as her feet remained rooted to the spot. Zach's grip tightened on her shoulders, and he drew closer to her, his warm body now pressed against hers.

"No," he bit out.

Evangeline shrugged. "Suit yourself."

In a move none of them saw coming, she grabbed Annabelle's arm and tore her from where she stood and sent her flying across the marble floor with remarkable strength her waif-like body didn't seem to possess. Annabelle's shoulder slammed into the wall, and pain made stars dance in front of her eyes.

"You're going to watch her die, Lover Boy," Evangeline continued with the gun now trained on Zach. She pulled something from her pocket, and when she aimed her hand towards Zach's ear, his whole body seized up.

Annabelle gasped with horror as a network of dark veins painted itself on the side of his face, and his body then went down like a dead weight. His eyes remained open, fixed on her where he now lay on the floor.

"No!" she screamed. That bitch couldn't have killed him.

"Oh, don't worry. He isn't dead. Yet," Evangeline said and added a little giggle at the end. "He's just paralyzed, but his mind is fully conscious, and all his senses are working just fine. He will enjoy watching this."

Annabelle gulped as a tear slid down her cheek. Zach ... The whole expanse of the living room was between them right now. Why the hell had she wanted such a big house?

"This should be fun," the blonde continued as she ditched the gun onto the sofa. She grimaced as she turned back to Annabelle. "Nasty things, guns. I personally don't like them, but they do the job when required." She gave a twisted, deranged grin. "Now, where were we?"

Annabelle swallowed with difficulty and lifted her gaze to her. "What do you want, you psycho?"

That ugly pout again.

"Me? Just what I'm due, dearie."

When she pulled out the thin, pointy dagger from the back of her jeans, fear made Annabelle freeze. Her whole body hurt from the sudden seizing, not unlike what had overtaken Zach.

"So, let's get started, shall we?"

The killer approached her, and a slash of her hand later, Annabelle winced when air entered the cut on her left arm.

"Now that's more like it." Evangeline went ahead with another slash, this time to Annabelle's ankle. "Do you know what *Lingshi* is? No, of course, you don't. Its translation is 'death by a thousand cuts'."

Slash—to the right shoulder.

"The Chinese emperor used to order it for all sorts of offences. Things such as high treason."

Slash—to her right calf this time.

Tears were now coursing down Annabelle's cheeks. The cuts were burning, the pain radiating slowly into the muscles as it seeped into her entire body. Move— she should move, do something. But she couldn't. Did the dagger have poison on its tip? Because she was immobile, the stinging of the cuts worked a sort of haze on her, sending her in shock.

She couldn't let that happen ... Zach ... Someone had to do something.

She had to do something!

"You know what I'm talking about, don't you, Annabelle?"

The blonde ripped the tip of the dagger on the chest this time, near the collarbone. The trickle of the blood up here was warm and gooey.

"See? Even your bodice is telling the truth, displaying the scarlet letter like so."

Indeed, the front of her gown was now turning dark with blood.

"He was mine!" Evangeline said with a furious scowl that instantly turned her from ethereally beautiful to something like a wicked witch in a fantasy TV show.

So that's what this was about—Dax deserting Evangeline for her.

"So you're going to die for it, and for making him turn on me. You, his precious angel who 'showed him the right path'." She said those words doing inverted commas in the air with her hands. "I had planned a slower, more poetic sending off for you, but Lover Boy here had to get involved."

She tsked and shook her head. The dagger ripped down to cut another line on Annabelle's thigh this time. "And he's going to watch. Then, when your blood is emptying itself from your body, he will be just conscious enough by then for me to get started with him in the same way. Just think. In death, both your blood will mingle on this pristine white marble floor. Star-crossed lovers united thus, but too late for them. How sad."

Zach ... Annabelle risked a glance at him. Their gazes locked, and in those deep brown eyes, she saw agony and desperation. He was aware of what was going on. Her heart broke for him.

"Let him go," she croaked.

She screamed when Evangeline rounded on her with two rapid cuts to the abdomen, tearing her dress in the process. The blonde then kicked her in the left side, so hard that she lost her breath. The crystals on the fabric got pushed into the open wound, making her see black for a second as the hurt overtook her.

This couldn't be happening! She had suffered worse beatings at the hands of her Krav Maga instructor. True, she had only been to the lessons twice, but still, she should've been made of sterner stuff. Unless ...

Unless this was it. Death. She had cheated it once, at the hands of this same woman.

She frowned as something registered in her mind. "You are ... the Harleys' nanny."

"Urgh. You wouldn't believe how much I had to keep my shit together when pretending to look after their snot-nosed brat, and that disgusting man with his lecherous paws."

No, she couldn't have hurt them, too. Not the baby. "You killed them?"

"What? Oh, no. Well, not yet, anyway. Had to take care of you two lovebirds first. But I'll go back there after I'm done here." She giggled. "Let's just say I will relieve Mr. Harley of a tiny—and I do mean tiny!— piece of his body."

Annabelle blinked as she stared up at her. What was it with killers already telegraphing all their moves to their victims? Did she get her kick out of the fear this made slither down the backs of her targets?

Another cut landed on her forearm, and she didn't even bother to cry or gasp this time. The pain built steadily in her left shoulder—she must've hit it harder than she'd thought upon contact with the wall. The end was near, anyway—best she used it doing something that would bring her a spark of joy, at least. The sight of Zach as the last thing she saw before she died would do it for her soul.

She furrowed her eyebrows when she glanced at him. Had the distance between them reduced? Could he be coming back into his strength?

She locked eyes with him, and he blinked. Yes, he seemed to be telling her something. He was moving.

If Evangeline found out, she would kill him on the spot. Annabelle couldn't let this happen. She had to do something. Anything. If Zach could get to the gun while she distracted the killer ...

"Kill me already," she muttered as she gazed up at the despicable creature, hissing at the debilitating pain gathering in her left shoulder.

Evangeline pouted again and came to crouch in front of Annabelle's prone body on the floor. She ran the tip of the dagger softly over her cheek, the pressure deepening as she trailed it down to the neck and started piercing the skin there.

"Where would be the fun in that?" the woman bent and whispered in her ear.

The killer would never get any closer than this ...

Annabelle didn't think; she only listened to instinct. She whipped her head forward. Her hair lifted with the momentum and slapped Evangeline in the face like a thousand little lashes. The blonde gave a little gasp of surprise, and when the dagger registered warm and stable in Annabelle's grip, she reached for it.

In the split-second when she caught it, and Evangeline relinquished her hold, their eyes met. The blonde even lifted an eyebrow as if daring her to do something.

Annabelle didn't even dare blink. She gripped the handle tight and slammed the blade sideways hard.

When the dagger anchored into something substantial and refused to budge, she let go, horror filling her as she eyed the blade now stuck into Evangeline's side.

The assassin blinked at her, an expression of astonishment on her features and horror in her eyes.

"Women don't stab," she said with disbelief heavy in her tone.

As if! If Annabelle had to do it again, she'd do it without a second thought.

She should finish this psycho before she caused any more damage, killed more innocent people. But bile rose up to her gorge as she stared at the knife from where it protruded out of the blonde's body. A part of her couldn't believe she had done it, and that part was quickly gaining ground.

She wouldn't be able to do it.

When Evangeline propped herself on an elbow and winced as she pulled the dagger from her side, Annabelle knew what would come next. The naked fury on the doll-like face was ugly to watch, and so would be the death she would wield.

"Fine," she threw out. "You get to see him die first, bitch."

She turned towards where Zach's body was ... but before she could complete the spin, the hand holding the dagger slammed into her own belly one-two-three-four times, held by Zach's large palm. As her body fell to the side, Zach dislodged the blade from her grip and spun it around to slash at her.

It happened too quickly for Annabelle to see him slit her throat open. The pool of her blood, however? It seemed to grow as if in slow motion.

Zach ... Fatigue was crashing over her now, a lingering pain flaring from her left shoulder, but she forced herself to angle her head in his direction.

He could still be the last thing she saw before she died ...

He crawled over to her. The network of dark veins on his face was almost gone by now. She tried to lift her arm so she could touch his strong jaw and hold on to it like a lifeline for the rest of time she had, but her hand fell with a limp plop when she attempted the move. It was also tiring her so much.

"Zach," she murmured, her eyes fluttering as she fought to keep them open.

"It's okay," he cooed. "I'm sending for help. Hold on. Please hold on, Annabelle."

She tried to, but it was a battle she was sorely losing.

"Hold me," she murmured.

As if in a dream, she felt him cradle her to his warm body. The heat diffused into her, chasing away the cold that however gained ground and continued spreading.

But he was holding her. She could let go now.

With a sigh, she closed her eyes and did just that.

CHAPTER NINE

Balaclava, Mauritius.
Saturday, February 21. 1.32 p.m.

Annabelle frowned when the intercom from the gate buzzed, letting her know she had a visitor. Not again. Rosalie Harley had dropped by the day before with her two-year-old, Tommy. The woman had heard from Mrs. DaSilva that Annabelle was in bad shape, and she had brought a casserole.

Annabelle had smiled politely as Rosalie had moaned about how her latest nanny had bailed on them and she would now have to find another. Not an easy feat given the way her husband's reputation for chasing blondes' knickers preceded him.

She had winced inside herself, reminded of Evangeline hiding there in plain sight all this time—how many times had she waved at her when they'd crossed paths on the streets?—and she had pretended to be tired, so the woman would leave. She had done the same thing with Mrs. DaSilva the day before. Whatever had happened to their quiet neighbourhood where nobody ever mingled?

If this were another do-gooder bringing food, she would pretend she wasn't here.

She frowned as she stared at the image from the camera to the side of the gate. It was a dark-haired man in a Range Rover. Jonathan.

What was he doing here?

Curiosity got the better of her, and she opened the gate remotely so he could come in. As she stepped onto the porch, she closed the long cardigan she was wearing over her body. She also had a turtleneck under, and the sun started a slow burn on her skin after a few seconds outside under its blinding rays. Inside, she powered the air conditioning on eighteen degrees Celsius so she could stay in the clothes. They concealed the many wounds on her body. A lot of the stitches hadn't yet fallen off, and she looked like Frankenstein's bride with all the sutures on her.

Jonathan smiled at her as he alighted from the vehicle.

"Hey," he said with his guileless, crooked smile.

She smiled back. "Hey yourself. I … I didn't think I'd see you again."

"Yeah. I wasn't here for the past week."

She furrowed her eyebrows. Why was he telling her this?

"You busy?" he asked.

She hugged the cardigan closer on her and threw a look over her shoulder at the house. She could lie and tell him she was busy, but—she'd never thought she'd say this—she had binge-watched just about everything she could binge-watch already on Netflix.

"Not really," she replied.

He nodded. "Care to come with me for an hour or two?"

"You abducting me or something?" She wouldn't put it past the lot, frankly.

He laughed. "I wouldn't have announced myself if I was."

True. The calm way he'd said this should've made her shiver, but she was past any surprise where he and the whole Corpus thing were concerned now.

"I'll grab my bag," she said, and went back in to do just that and set the alarm before she closed the front door.

Once in the vehicle, she buckled up and laughed softly when the music player started as he turned the engine on. Seemed Jonathan was a soft rock fan.

A far cry from Zach …

She slammed the lid down on the thought, but the hurt had still had time to slither its way into her.

The last time she had seen Zach had been before she'd passed out in her house after he had killed Evangeline. They said he had stayed by her side for a few hours before he'd had to leave. She had still been unconscious then.

She had woken up in a bed inside a luxurious private clinic. Her Aunt Annette had been by her bedside, informing her it was midday on Friday the thirteenth already. She had been in and out of consciousness for over thirty hours. She'd been brought in suffering from acute loss of blood which had put her into hypovolemic shock, and the doctors had diagnosed a tear in her spleen needing surgery. It had been touch and go because her blood pressure had refused to stabilize.

Maybe because she had decided she wouldn't keep on fighting for her life? Her first thought when she had opened her eyes had been, "What now?" This had made her think of Zach. She hadn't asked about him, but Simmi, who came in soon after and switched places with Aunt Annette, told her Zach had had superficial injuries from the car accident.

So that's how they had covered it all. To this day, she still didn't know how they had pulled it off. The question had plagued her as she'd spent close to a week inside the most expensive private clinic on the island. Daniel had told her Wexler-Prinsloo had insisted on footing the bill because the accident had happened as she had been taking their representative, Zach, to the airport that early morning. The Jaguar F-Pace rental she had apparently been driving had been written off as a total loss after the accident, which had supposedly happened on a stretch of motorway known as La Vigie. The area always made her think of those eerie roads going through cold, fog-filled forests in Canada.

Aunt Annette and Uncle Brian had done their best to coax her to stay at their house in Grand Baie—their place looked like a villa from the five-star resorts they owned, opening onto a pristine beach in the region known as the Mauritian Côte d'Azur. But she had wanted to come home, more so to see how Simmi couldn't have noticed anything amiss as she'd been looking after the cats for her during her stay in the clinic.

The headboard had been replaced in her bedroom, she'd found, and aside from the shag-pile rug in front of the sofa in the living room appearing a bit more grey and blue, the house had looked the same. No trace of any fight or assassination attempt. No speck of blood.

Who had organized the clean-up? Zach? Jonathan?

She risked a glance at him, and he must've felt gaze because he turned and glanced her way.

"Should I be afraid of what's waiting for me?" she asked him

He laughed. "My wife can be scary at times, but no. You don't have to worry."

His wife. He was taking her to his place?

She blinked as she recognized being on the West coast of the island now, in the expat hub of Rivière

Noire. Those nearby mountains didn't lie. That's where he lived?

Indeed, he turned into a tree-lined driveway opening onto a gravel-filled courtyard in front of a well-restored, one-storey colonial residence. He stopped the Range Rover and indicated for her to get out. She frowned when she stepped out and saw the five-foot-tall barriers in front of all the opened French windows on the porch.

He led the way up the half-dozen, cut stone stairs and eased a barrier from the main door, closing it again behind her once she had stepped inside.

The sound of squeaky thumps caught her attention, and her frown turned into a grin when she saw the little boy who rushed up to Jonathan screaming "Papa!" as he jumped into the man's arms.

Jonathan laughed and hugged his son, then turned to Annabelle.

Her eyes went wide as she saw the two of them so up close. The kid looked exactly like his father, from the chestnut hair, fair skin, to the china doll blue eyes. And he had the same crooked smile, too.

"This is Anthony," Jonathan said. "Say hello to Annabelle, lad."

"'Ello," he said, giving her a toothy smile.

Such a sunny child. He must be the light of Jonathan's life.

"He decided not to nap today," a female voice said.

"Mamma, doggy," the child said as he lurched in his father's arms towards where his mother was coming from.

The woman picked the boy up with ease from Jonathan's arms, as if this were a dance they had choreographed and performed so many times, it was now muscle memory.

"Not going to see the doggy today, Anthony," she told him.

His little face grew crestfallen, and Annabelle expected him to bawl next. But he surprised her by looking up at his mother and giving her a bright smile.

"Car?" he asked.

His mum kissed him on the cheek, then placed him on his feet. He wasted no time careening away inside the house.

Ah, so that's what the barriers were about. Kid protection devices.

"You must be this Annabelle I hear so much about."

She turned to Jonathan's wife and paused for a split-second to take her in. The woman was tall and thin, with dusky skin, long and straight black hair, and dark doe eyes. Her accent had sounded entirely British, just like Jonathan's, but Annabelle would place her as having South Indian origins.

"I'm Melinda," she said as she reached forward and embraced Annabelle.

Annabelle was stunned for a second, and Melinda let her go.

"I'm sorry. Did I hurt you?"

She blinked. Did she know? She looked to Jonathan, who nodded.

So Melinda must also be working for the Corpus, then, to be aware of what had happened so far.

She shook herself under the worried look Melinda was still sending her. "Oh, no. No. I'm sorry. I was just a bit stunned, I suppose."

Melinda smiled at her. "It's nice to finally meet you."

"I would say the same, but I didn't know you existed. I mean, I knew Jonathan was married from the wedding band on his finger, sure, but ...” Why was she babbling so much? “It’s nice to meet you, too.”

Jonathan came up to Annabelle and placed a gentle hand on her shoulder. “There’s someone here you also need to meet.”

For a second, her heart had started hammering, grabbing on to hope. But Jonathan had said ‘meet’—this was someone she didn’t know.

It couldn’t be Zach, then.

As much as it killed her not to know what had become of him, his mission was over, and therefore, he’d gone out of her life. So she quelled the urge to ask one more time and forced a bright smile onto her face.

“Lead the way,” she told him.

He started towards the back of the house. She threw only a cursory glance at the period furniture from the East India Company all around her. When they reached the conservatory, her step halted on the threshold at the sight of a man standing by the window opening onto the full expanse of the back garden done in rolling English style.

Jonathan gave her shoulder a gentle squeeze, and then he left her there.

The man turned to her. He was breathtakingly handsome, with long dark hair and clear-cut features that spoke of maturity and wisdom despite the fact he couldn’t be older than early forties. His eyes, though—they looked like captivating emeralds.

“Annabelle,” he said in a deep, rumbling voice. “You don’t mind if I call you by your Christian name, I hope?”

Something momentous was about to happen—she could feel it vibrating in her every cell.

She shook her head. “I don’t mind. You’re friend, not foe.”

His eyebrows rose. "Straight to the point. I like it."

He gestured towards the rattan sofas with overstuffed floral cushions on them. She went ahead and sat down on one. He settled opposite her.

"My name is Graeme," he said.

She concealed the frown wanting to make its presence known on her face as she saw him up close. He seemed familiar.

"I won't beat around the bush," he started. "Jonathan, Melinda, and I work together."

So this was what this was about. She hitched in a breath. "For the Corpus, you mean."

The hint of a smile touched his lips. "Indeed. You've heard of it."

She nodded.

"It has been brought to our attention that you would make a formidable addition to our ranks."

She gulped. By who? Zach?

"You know what we are about?" he asked as he fixed his deep green gaze on her.

"Ideology. Meaning in the service of power."

"And said power belongs to?"

She shrugged. "No one per se. You work as the stealthy left hand who gets things done wherever and whenever needed."

"Very good. I'm impressed."

He'd said he liked her being direct—she didn't have it in her to pussy-foot around anymore. Life was too precious to waste it, as the past two weeks had shown her.

"You wish to recruit me?"

"Yes."

He didn't seem surprised she had taken the lead. Good. It told her it wasn't an autocratic system inside their organization.

Zach had mentioned the actual leader of the agency had recruited him. Could Graeme be the new leader now? She blinked. No, he'd said the man's daughter had taken the reins.

"Doing what?" she asked.

"Little things." He shrugged. "Keeping an ear to the ground. Passing on information and gathering some more along the way. Maybe instigate a little rumour from time to time."

She smiled. "That's what I do just about every day in PR, you know?"

He smiled back. "Exactly. You'd be a natural."

She narrowed her gaze onto him. She did do that, among other things, day in and day out at her job, but this wouldn't be harmless stuff like purposefully letting leak how a world-renowned DJ was contemplating mixing for an upcoming dance festival at a five-star hotel.

"How dangerous would it get?" she asked.

"You'll be trained, of course. But let us say you've already faced the worst of what this clandestine life has to offer. The waters will not even seem choppy compared to what you've known."

He meant Evangeline.

"What's in it for me?" she asked.

"Doing the right thing?"

She cocked an eyebrow at him.

"It pays very well," he added.

Far from her to be spitting on money well-earned, but it wasn't her motivation. She recalled Zach's words from that fateful night. She, too, was looking for purpose. She'd thought Sparkle would be it, but when weighing event management to please a select few against the fact she could actively be working towards world peace all while doing exactly what she'd been doing so far? Who wouldn't take such an opportunity?

"It's not an easy decision to make," he stated.

She heard the sound of laughter in the house. Melinda and Anthony.

Her heart squeezed in her chest. Jonathan and Melinda had a family, a life together, and that worked because they belonged to the same agency, with no secrets and no lies between them. If she joined the Corpus, a part of her life would always have to remain partitioned off, never to be shared with a 'civilian', aka anyone not from the organization.

Could she do it? She wanted love later. A family.

But then, she bit her lip. Look at her track record with love. It was pathetic, really.

Maybe the highest she could reach now was in a professional capacity, both at Sparkle and with the Corpus. What else did she have waiting for her?

Certainly, no man. Not Zach ...

She shook the thought of him away and trained her attention onto Graeme.

"I'm in."

He watched her for long seconds. Then, he nodded. When he stood, she followed suit.

"Welcome to the Corpus," he said as he put out his right hand.

She clasped it and shook for good measure.

As if conjured by magic, Melinda appeared in the doorway. "Tea?"

It must be close to three o'clock. Everyone on the island took tea at that time—they had the Brits beaten where this tradition was concerned.

"You'll have to excuse me, Mel," Graeme said. "I have to catch the plane back to Prague."

Melinda's smile fell. "You'll have to visit some other time."

"I will." He turned in Annabelle's direction. "Maybe now we have new blood …"

Melinda gasped and brought a hand to cover her mouth. "You took the offer!"

Annabelle nodded as Graeme exited the room, conferring with Jonathan who held a squirming Anthony in his arms. The man ruffled the little boy's hair, then made his way out of the dwelling.

"Jonathan, she joined!" Melinda exclaimed as her husband came in.

He smiled at them. "Welcome to the Corpus. There's a lot you have to learn now."

Annabelle frowned as she watched him. "You're going to teach me?"

"Just been given the task by the big man himself."

When she thought back to Graeme, and putting together everything she knew so far about the agency, a light bulb went off in her head. She gasped.

"Wait a minute. That man is Graeme Whitman. The baby daddy of Alexis Friedrich."

Their photos graced tabloids and gossip magazines almost every week—the reason why he'd seemed familiar. And Zach had mentioned the leader of the Corpus being killed and his daughter stepping in … said daughter who had sent this man to recruit her … The pieces fell into place.

"Oh. My. God! The Corpus is run by *Dynamogenics* heiress Alexis Friedrich?" she exclaimed.

Melinda just laughed and took her elbow. "And you don't even know the half of it! Have you heard about the mutiny? It was Alexis' biological mother who was responsible …"

As Melinda prattled on and led her to a salon where tea awaited them, Annabelle quelled her surprise and took a deep breath. She had just entered another universe, it seemed.

***

Berlin, Germany. Grunewald neighbourhood in the Charlottenburg-Wilmersdorf borough
Sunday, February 22. 3.05 p.m.

Zach never failed to lose his breath every time he saw this house. Well, *house* was putting it mildly. This was a gothic *Schönbrunn* replica. The palace of Empress Sissi in Vienna had a golden look to it, sure, but even the dark walls and small windows here couldn't hide the eerie similarity.

The frozen-solid ground crunched under his booted feet as though he were walking on crisp sugar cookies. He had trouble imagining this was a green and thick lawn during summertime. He shivered under the cold, rubbing his gloved hands together to stop them from freezing over.

From where she sat on a bench farther up, Alexis watched him and laughed.

"To think you trained in this city," she chided.

He cursed as he joined her. She had a thick red wool coat on, only the rosy flush on her cheeks indicating she was feeling the cold, too.

"That was in spring," he muttered as he sat down by her side.

She laughed again. Silence settled when the sound died.

"It's done?" she asked softly without looking at him.

He clamped his jaw. "Yes."

The intel from Dax Vosloo's USB stick had actually given them Evangeline's true identity. She had been Vanya Ivanova, an orphan who had displayed marked psychopathic tendencies in the Moscow orphanage where she had grown up. The authorities had sent her to Siberia when she was ten, and it went to show how dangerous and twisted she was that the SVR had passed on recruiting her to join them.

At sixteen, Vanya had murdered her way out of the orphanage, an escape spree where she had killed every guard who had stood in her way using her bare hands and instruments like pebbles and paper clips. She had loitered around Russia for a few years until the day Alexis' biological mother had stumbled upon her and started to groom her to be the Kali of her rogue Corpus.

Knowing her identity had enabled them to draw some connecting dots around some of her kills. They had uncovered many more thanks to Vosloo's precise record-keeping, and this had painted the picture of her actual network.

Over the past nine days, he had chased a lead in Thailand, which had then led him to Singapore, the Philippines, Cairo, and finally, Kinshasa. Vosloo had been on the right track, though he, too, hadn't known of the extent of Evangeline's net across the Asian and African continents.

The network creator had been taken into Corpus custody the day before in the capital of the Democratic Republic of Congo. He now awaited in a cell down in the dungeon of this same castle behind him. Alexis' residence.

"Thank you, Zachariah."

"No need."

He was like a father to me, too. He didn't say it out loud, though, but Alexis must've heard the words.

"He would've been proud of you."

Zach simply nodded.

It was over and done now. They had to look to the future, consolidating the bases of the new, improved Corpus.

"Where do you want me next?" he asked.

"About that ..."

He waited with bated breath. Was she keeping him in this cold as Hades land with her? All her close collaborators worked in her entourage here.

"You never wanted ... more?" she asked without looking at him.

His dutiful instinct told him to rush on and say no. But something else whispered she wasn't talking to him as the boss now, but as close to a friend as she could get.

A sad smile touched his almost-frozen lips, making it feel like a rictus. "There was a time ... Yes."

A perfect night with a beautiful woman, when they had danced around a room like that night was their only night.

The memory of what had happened next flitted in, and his hands tightened into fists. His heart had almost stopped when he had seen Evangeline in the living room, and then, he'd been paralyzed but conscious, able to see and know how much Annabelle was suffering from the psycho's warped revenge.

He'd been lucky, though. Evangeline hadn't had the dedicated earplugs to negate the effects of the sonic taser she had used on him. As such, she had powered the device next to his ear for only a few seconds, and he'd been able to recover soon after. If she'd used it for the necessary one-minute interval, he would've been out of commission for more than ten minutes. Ample time for the assassin to have done her dirty work.

He hadn't thought twice before killing her. No, Annabelle had been too important. She had been hurt … there had been so much blood … He'd sent for Dr. Berger, and the older man had gotten in just in time to start an O-neg transfusion and then rush her to the clinic.

Jonathan and a crew had taken care of setting up the cover story, and a few hands greased at the clinic and with the authorities had made the report state what they wanted: Annabelle had suffered from a ruptured spleen and the many cuts after a devastating traffic collision. Him? It was a miracle he had escaped the accident unscathed.

He didn't remember living in the hours when she had been in surgery. Then, he'd stayed by her bedside despite all the glares from the staff as she'd been wheeled to ICU, her blood pressure refusing to stabilize given how much blood she had already lost on top of the internal bleeding the injury had triggered.

On the dot of four o'clock that Thursday, the news had come—Gaia had broken through the encryption on the USB key, and they now had Evangeline's identity. He'd had to leave her side then to answer the call of duty.

"If you could have the chance, would you take it?" Alexis asked, tearing him out of his recollections.

It didn't take long for him to come up with an answer, but at the same time, it took a considerable time for the feelings to settle and show him the path.

It had killed him to leave her side as she had lain there unconscious, the skin of her body almost disappearing under all the bandages covering the sutures, the doctors trying to sew together the many cuts that had been inflicted onto her.

"Yes. I would."

But it wouldn't happen. Not in their world. His allegiance was to the Corpus, and frankly, it was all he knew how to be. A soldier took orders and followed diligently. He had chosen this life. To make a difference. To make his own existence matter.

"It was your purpose."

Annabelle's words flittered into his mind, and he closed his eyes hard as he fought the thought of her away. Too bad he couldn't shrug off the dead weight that seemed to crush down on his chest now.

"Then you can have it," Alexis said softly.

Zach blinked. Had he heard her right?

"I beg your pardon?"

She turned to face him then, a wistful smile on her face. "It was the choice he gave all his case officers before he died."

Her father. Romantic entanglements, especially with civilians, had been a strict no-no inside the agency in the past.

"It's the one I'm giving you now," she continued.

He blinked as he processed the words. "Wait, you said this applies to your case officers. I'm just an agent."

"Not anymore. Not if you choose to, that is." She looked the other way now, her gaze lost in the distance. "The spy game is no longer what it was in Africa, and you know it. Russia is the new man at the helm, France having been pushed off the chessboard almost completely. African leaders choose to employ

Israeli protection officers or contractors when they need a job done. And when you add the Chinese making eyes at the continent … We need to up our game now."

He nodded at her accurate assessment, but a part of him still reeled from the offer she had placed on the table. To be a case officer meant he would be less in the field, yes, but he would have agents working under him. He would be the one doing the strategizing and overseeing all missions.

Logically, it was the next step he could aspire to. But he'd thought such an opportunity would come in another decade or so. He should jump on this promotion.

"When do I leave for Djibouti?"

***

Port-Louis, Mauritius. St Georges Street
Monday, February 23. 9.08 a.m.

"*Patronne!* What are you doing here?"
Annabelle winced as Daniel faffed around her like a mother hen when she stepped foot inside the Sparkle premises that morning. When she saw Haseena converging on her, she ducked into her office as quickly as her still hurting body would allow and closed the door in the woman's face.

She grimaced when loud bangs started on the panel.

"You're supposed to be resting!" Haseena yelled from the other side.

If she saw the walls of her house non-stop for another day, she would lose her shit. She'd had it up to here with being cooped up whether at home or at

Simmi's place. The only redeeming thing she could hang on to was the newfound friendship with Melinda, who was going to teach her the ropes of self-defence and then how to attack and disarm, maim, or even kill if she had to.

She had been surprised to find the woman had actually been a detective in the London Metropolitan Police before she joined the Corpus.

Because of her spleen injury and the subsequent surgery, she would have to wait another three months before she could engage in any vigorous physical activity. She also had to contend with the risk of triggering a hernia in the same time frame if she tried lifting heavy things.

That bitch of Evangeline had really done a number on her.

At the anger flaring in her, she closed her eyes, took a deep breath, and allowed herself to feel the full force of her rage for the count of seven. After that, she inhaled even deeper, shrugged her shoulders and neck, then opened her eyes and shook her arms and hands.

Far from her to be able to or even want to forgive the psychopath for what she'd done, but Annabelle had no place and indeed no time in her life for such negativity. This technique worked great to allow her to get her kick out of any emotion but not let it get the better of her.

She stared at the closed door, then with a sigh, opened the panel just a crack. Haseena still stood outside, and Annabelle simply stared at her without saying a word.

After a few minutes, the turbaned woman grimaced. "Business as usual?"

Annabelle nodded. "Business as usual."

She opened the door wide then went to her desk. Daniel came in to hand her the folder for Margot Dupuis' pop-up store venture, and she fell onto it like a junkie starved of her crack.

"Annabelle!"

She glanced up when Daniel skidded to a halt against the doorway. She even winced as he slammed into the wood frame.

"It's ... you ... I ..." he blabbered.

What the hell? She started getting up, and the booming voice outside in the hallway froze her mid-movement.

"You're one hard woman to meet."

She peered up, and her legs almost gave way under her when she spotted the Yves Saint Laurent-lookalike strolling into her office wearing a dark suit, the glinting cufflinks on his sleeves obviously diamonds.

"Sir," she muttered.

He waved a hand in the air.

"Oh, none of that between us. Call me Simon." He turned towards Daniel, who had flattened himself against the wall to let him pass. "Excuse me, young man."

He then closed the door to her office and marched to her desk. He reached for her hand and shook it hard before undoing the button in his suit jacket and sitting down in the visitor's chair.

Annabelle was still hovering halfway up from her chair, and she sat down with a plop, too stunned to attend to decorum right then.

"I have been twiddling my thumbs for a whole weekend in one of those overdone hotels on the coasts, waiting for you to pop up at your office again."

"Oh, I … I'm sorry. I …" She stopped herself from saying she'd been in an accident.

He waved his hand again. "Never mind. You're here now. Let's get this show on the road."

She frowned. "What show, if I may ask?"

True, she must be coming across as a dimwit in front of *the* Simon Wexler. The man seemed to be taking it in stride, though. Probably used to people being bulldozed by his exuberant manner and charismatic presence.

"The partnership, of course." He reached into the inside pocket of his suit, but didn't seem to find what he was looking for.

"James!" he then barked, making Annabelle flinch.

A second later, a knock came at the door. A harried young man stepped in with a sheaf of papers in his hand. Without a word, he gave those to Simon and made his exit.

Simon perused the first page then flipped the stack over to her. She gingerly reached for it.

"Conditions of the agreement. In short, you access the Wexler-Prinsloo network, and all our resources and contacts are yours. We get the same from you in return, and of course, there will be someone from our house who will be sent to work with you as a liaison."

"Sounds fair enough," she heard herself saying.

Who would they be sending? Maybe Zach …? But then, she remembered the Wexler-Prinsloo rep thing had been his cover to get close to her.

Simon Wexler had narrowed his gaze onto her, and she squirmed under the intensity.

"Just so you know," he started. "You won this deal fair and square, based on the merits of your work ethic and the track record of your agency." He paused. "Not because of …"

He didn't add anything further, and she frowned, not picking the hint. Then, it all came together. Wexler-Prinsloo was a front for the Corpus—she wasn't winning this partnership as compensation for what had happened to her.

"You mean?" she ventured to ask.

He nodded. "Yes. That."

No one, it seemed, wanted to say Evangeline. She must have become the new 'that which shall not be named.'

"John and I had our eyes on your outfit for a while," he added.

Come to think of it, *she* worked for the Corpus now.

"My answer is yes," she told him.

He nodded towards the papers still in her grip. "Look it over before you sign. The clauses are binding."

"I will."

He stood, then, and she followed suit, sending silent thanks out that she hadn't tumbled her chair back or snagged her trousers or something along the edge.

"I'll have a courier pick those up in two hours," he stated.

"It will be ready," she told him.

"Good. Ms. De Castelban? Welcome to Wexler-Prinsloo."

He shook her hand, then walked out of her office with the same exuberance with which he'd arrived. She remained in stunned silence for a full minute, and no one even peered into her office. They must be as astounded as she was.

Then all Hell broke loose as Haseena and Daniel both tried to rush into the room at the same time.

"What happened?" they asked, breathless.

She gazed at them, blinking when she saw the rest of the staff behind them in the hallway.

"Simon Wexler just made us his," she mumbled, still under shock, too.

No one said a word for a full five seconds, then a cacophony of cheers and whoops erupted. Daniel rushed in and hugged her. When she winced as her wounds were still sensitive, he released her and profusely apologized.

"So, does it mean we get a raise?" Haseena asked.

Annabelle narrowed her gaze on her. "Dream on."

The agreement would inevitably not involve financial aid, too.

"The afternoon off, then?" Deepika asked.

She rolled her eyes.

"Priorities, people! We have the pop-up store to set up." She clapped her hands and waved them away. "Dinner and drinks on me tonight at Le Suffren. But right now, back at work. Chop chop!"

She settled back down at the desk, pulled the contract to her, and went over it with a fine-toothed comb. Two hours later, when the courier indeed came to pick it up, she returned the signed document with him and settled back with the pop-up store file. They did have their work cut out for them, what with her having lost over a week with her injuries.

"Annabelle! *Patronne!*"

She sighed without looking up from the papers. She doubted another sensational appearance had graced the lobby. Lightning didn't strike twice.

"What is it, Daniel?"

"I was hoping someone would need a tall drink of water."

The pen dropped from her hand. No, she couldn't have heard that voice. What was he doing here?

Slowly, she forced herself to look up, preparing herself to be disappointed when she would realize she had, again, imagined him in her midst. She hated the painkillers the doctors had her on because they sometimes made her see things. But wait, she hadn't taken any this morning—she had forgotten, remembering only once in the car on the way here, stuck in the morning traffic jam to get into the capital.

So this couldn't be a hallucination. He really stood there, leaning to the side with his shoulder against the frame, his arms crossed over his chest. The tailored ink-blue suit hugged every line of his well-defined body, and she finally glanced up into his face, finding his so-kissable lips in a wide smile.

"What ..." she murmured. "What are you doing here?"

"I came to see you." He shrugged. "See if you might need my help around."

Behind him, she could see the curious vultures named Daniel and Haseena hanging on to every word they were saying. She wanted to get up in a flash and go slam the door in their face, but she winced even as she stood.

The smile slipped from Zach's face, and he had reached her side in three long strides.

"Talk to me. What's wrong?" he asked, clasping her shoulders, worry now evident on his face.

She shook her head. "Just the general and prolonged business of healing."

His eyes grew stormy. "I am so sorry about that."

She nodded, then something made her glance at the door again. Those two were still there. She shrugged away from Zach's touch and went to the door, which she closed. She then turned back to him.

"What happened?" she asked. "After ..."

His jaw clamped. "I wanted to stay with you. Believe me when I tell you I didn't want to leave your side at the hospital."

Her heart clenched at the naked hurting he didn't bother to hide in his tone.

"You had things to do. I understand." She paused. "They done?"

He nodded.

She hitched in a breath. Could she ask him this? Should she?

She licked her lips and inhaled deeply.

"What now?" she asked.

"You just signed the Wexler-Prinsloo agreement."

"Yes."

"There's something in it saying they will appoint someone to work here?"

She frowned. No, this couldn't be right.

"That's ... you?" she finally managed to utter.

"Stuck with me, sadly. Like white on rice."

A giggle left her when he said those words, and she winced. It hurt. Oh, hell, it hurt so much. She hadn't laughed since the accident, thus had had no clue how this would feel.

He came up to her and took her hand to lead her to the settee in the corner, where they both sat down.

"Long story short, Sparkle's presence on the island will be more than a front for the Corpus. Alexis wants this to be a satellite office to the Djibouti main bureau. Mauritius is the ideal stepping stone between Africa and Asia. It would be remiss if she didn't exploit this platform."

Cold doused her heart. This was Corpus business—that was why he had come back. He'd mentioned Djibouti, where he used to work before.

Annabelle lowered her head. She wouldn't be able to stand it to have him here so close to her and then lose him all over again. She had almost died before she'd stepped into the house that fateful morning to find Evangeline had been waiting for them—when she had realized how he had become her whole world while she had simply been a satellite in his orbit, their paths never meant to cross again.

"Hey," he coaxed, a hand under her chin. "What's wrong?

She blinked as she looked up into his narrowed eyes. "Where will you be based?"

He didn't reply for long seconds during which her heart sank even further.

"Here," he finally said. "With you. If you'll have me."

Her lips parted, but no sound came out.

"I don't understand," she finally said.

"I am in charge of the new cell here, Annabelle. Alexis made me a case officer. Jonathan, Melinda, you, and I are supposed to work together from here on."

A tear slipped down her cheek. Work. That's what it was.

"Don't cry," he said softly. "What did I do wrong? Please tell me."

She shook her head. "You did nothing wrong. It's me who ..."

Who has been an utter idiot, thinking anything good could happen to her heart.

"I don't ever want to see you cry," he said softly as he brushed the tear from her cheek with the pad of his thumb.

"Zach, I—"

"No, let me talk. Please."

She gazed up at him with blurry eyes.

"I was an arse. For treating you like I have. I should have stayed. I wanted to stay."

"But you couldn't."

"Not then."

Something dawned inside her. He was trying to tell her something.

"And you can now?" she asked, lower lip trembling as she said the words.

He rubbed the pad of his thumb on her cheek to clear away another tear.

"I can, and I want to. God only knows how much I want to."

She blinked as she watched him. He had come back to her.

Only one way to find out.

"Kiss me," she told him.

He sighed. "I thought you'd never ask."

When his lips touched hers, fire burst to life inside her, chasing away the cold and settling delicious warmth in its place. The taste of Zach fulfilled her, the feel of his mouth on hers, of his arms gently closing around her, bringing her home.

She broke away, panting. He pressed his forehead to hers, his breath coming as raggedly as hers.

A sliver of doubt still lingered in her heart.

"Zach," she asked, eyes closed. "Is this real?"

He kissed the tip of her nose. "As real as it's ever gonna get."

The conviction was steadfast in his voice, and when he kissed her this time, the cold left every single cell. Heat suffused her so fast, she had to tear herself from him to fan her face.

"I might, after all, need that tall glass of water," she told him with a giggle. "Ouch."

He smiled, holding her with tenderness and love. "At your service, Ms. de Castelban."

THE END

ABOUT ZEE MONODEE

From always choosing the storytelling option in English & French classes to sneaking a Mills&Boon romance under the desk at school, Zee went on to make a career out of writing the kind of emotional romances all young girls junk on.

Her Mauritius and Indian-based romances have all the classic makings of Bollywood-type drama: overbearing mothers, matchmaking aunties, 'proper' eligible suitors who look like frogs, race & class divides.

Travel to the UK (London, Surrey, & North Yorkshire), and you meet people—young and more mature—struggling to find 'The One' amid the drudgery of day-to-day life, never mind if they're a simple graphic designer working from home, a world-renowned supermodel battling anorexia, or a reluctant heiress on the run.

Take to the Corpus Agency mantle, and become lethal spies & assassins who nevertheless feel the call of love in their dark and shady lives...

Shadow Bridge, the UF series she co-writes with her BFF Natalie G. Owens, has a wide cast of mystical, magical, & mythological creatures trying to save the world from an impending Apocalypse.

Of Indian heritage & a 2x breast cancer survivor, Zee lives in paradise (aka Mauritius!) with her long-suffering husband, their smart-mouth teenage son, and their tabby cat who thinks herself a fearsome feline from the nearby African Serengeti plains. When she isn't in her kitchen rolling out chapattis or baking cakes while singing along to the latest pop hit topping the charts, she can be found reading or catching up on her numerous TV show addictions. In her day job, she is an editor who helps other authors like her hone their works and craft.

Connect with Zee: http://www.zeemonodee.com/

Thank you for reading Unravelling His Mark by Zee Monodee. If you enjoyed this book, please leave a review.

Continue reading for an excerpt from Healing His Medic by Nana Prah, The Protectors, Book 1.

CHAPTER ONE

The dead weight of Navy Commander Akin Solarin's naval brother in his arms didn't keep him from running towards the hospital. Despite the strain in his legs and the burn in his chest, he didn't stop for one second. Ishaq Obatola had squeezed himself into a tight ball, moaning in agony while they'd been sailing on the dinghy from their destroyer, Reckoning. Akin's own stomach had clenched with sympathetic pain and worry. Such moaning couldn't spell anything minor.

Waiting for a helicopter to reach their ship for an emergency transport would've wasted critical hours. When they had landed on the shores of The Gambia, they'd ordered a taxi to get them to the hospital with great haste.

Bursting through the doors of the Emergency Room, Akin spotted an empty stretcher and lay his friend onto it. Ishaq groaned as he rolled onto his side and tucked his knees to his chest.

"We need help. Help us!" he bellowed.

The four other officers who'd escorted them off the ship looked around the empty space and joined in the call, pushing open doors in search of someone. Anyone.

A woman came running through a pair of double doors that one of his men had yelled into. Her gaze darted around the room in alarm. Once they fell on the man curled up on the stretcher, she propelled into motion, reaching for a gown from a shelf and slipping it on in the few steps it took to reach them. "What happened?"

Did it matter? His best friend was in agony. Taking a breath, Akin drew on logic. "He said he's been feeling unwell and complained of severe pain in the lower part of his abdomen. On the ship, he said it might be his appendix and insisted that he had plenty of time before he'd have to see a doctor."

As the medic put on a mask with a plastic shield attached, two more hospital workers arrived. A pair of gloves completed the first woman's outfit before she rushed to the stretcher, where she placed two fingers along the side of Ishaq's neck. "What's his name?"

"Ishaq Obatola."

"Mr. Obatola, can you hear me?"

Without opening his eyes, he groaned before mumbling, "Appendix."

"That's for us to determine. Let's roll him into the examination room," she said in a crisp British accent that meant business.

Akin followed the squeaky stretcher through the swinging doors into a semi-private room. "It's Doctor Obatola."

The woman snapped her gaze up to Akin. "A medical doctor?"

He nodded. "Yes. So he should know what he's talking about."

"Dr. Obatola, I need you to lie on your back for me," the woman coaxed.

He could only presume her to be the doctor from the way she'd taken control and everyone else deferred to her.

She and another fully protected worker helped Ishaq onto his back while someone else took his temperature and blood pressure. Akin admired their ability to work as a tight-knit team.

Her fingers hovered over Ishaq's belly. "I'm going to palpate your abdomen."

Ishaq tried to draw his legs up in an attempt to prevent the woman from touching his belly. He drew in a breath before opening his lids to look at the doctor with bloodshot eyes. "Right lower quadrant pain," he mumbled.

"The rebound tenderness will make me pass out," he added after a deep grunt. "I'll give up my license if it isn't an appendicitis. It hit me too fast. Ultrasound, no time for X-ray. Surgery."

He then closed his eyes, his breaths harsh and fast.

The doctor considered him for a moment before turning her head to one of her staff. "Sara, please bring the ultrasound machine."

Akin's heart slowed its pounding as his esteem of her went up. She'd decided to listen to her patient rather than her ego.

"Blood pressure is ninety over sixty, pulse one-twenty, respirations forty. Temp is thirty-nine," the only male attending to Ishaq read out as he wrote on a paper.

The person she'd sent for the ultrasound came sliding to a halt with the equipment.

The doctor set up the machine. "I'm going to need you to lie flat so I can scan you."

Ishaq swallowed hard, and with a strength Akin admired, did as she asked. Clenched fists and jaw were the only signs his friend showed of being in pain as the doctor did her work.

She spoke directly to Ishaq when the grey picture came on the screen. "We're taking you to surgery, Dr. Obatola. You're abdomen is filled with fluid."

"Burst."

"Yes, your appendix has ruptured. Monica, alert the surgical team of an emergency appendectomy. Tariq, draw blood for a complete blood count, type, cross and match."

Akin gripped the edge of the trolley as terror squeezed the air out of his chest. He'd prefer taking out a slew of enemies in battle rather than seeing someone he considered a brother die.

The doctor touched Akin's shoulder. Warmth and a tingle made its way along his arm.

"We'll take good care of him."

Her reassuring grin alleviated a fraction of his trepidation. The awareness of her as more than a medical personnel did not.

CHAPTER TWO

Exhausted, with eyes too gritty to keep open without effort, and sipping on lukewarm coffee, Doctor Comfort Djan stepped into the long hallway. Her walk towards the testosterone-crowded waiting room set her belly quivering. The overpowering presence of the men had weighed on her as they'd watched her every move in the Emergency Room.

The surgery she'd assisted Dr. Peters with had taken hours longer than expected. She'd heard of doctors not taking care of themselves—hell, she could plead guilty—but she didn't think it was the case with her patient. Things had gone wrong for him too quickly to control.

She didn't look forward to updating the group of Dr. Obatola's condition. She should've opted to review the patients for Dr. Peters instead.

Hovering outside the door of the waiting room, she assessed the group. She'd never considered a man in a military uniform sexy, but these guys made her reconsider. Each stood as a mountain on his own, but the one she'd spoken to in the Emergency Room snagged her attention. Everything about him screamed leader. Guardian.

From his intense deep brown eyes, which complimented his golden skin, to his broad chin. She'd noticed the flare of his upturned nostrils when he'd heard something he didn't like. His firm lips had stayed pressed together as he'd given a curt nod when he'd been told that his friend had to be rushed to the operating room.

As if sensing her, the man raised his head and went from seated to standing at a height of what had to be six-foot-two in one lithe movement. The others followed.

She walked up to him, attempting to stay just far enough away so she wouldn't have to crane her neck in order to glance past the darkened shadow of stubble covering his strong jaw and into his expectant eyes.

Flanked by his men, she mentally reinforced that this was her domain, not theirs. "Mr..."

Had she learned his name? No.

"Akin."

"Mr. Akin—"

"No, just Akin. How is he?"

She clasped her hands in front of her and squeezed. "Dr. Obatola made it through the surgery."

The collective sigh of relief warmed the air.

She held up a hand to provide the rest of her news. "Not only had the appendix ruptured, but he had a diffuse infection of the peritoneum. When—"

"You just operated on the only man among us who could've understood what you just said."

Akin's scowl disturbed her. How could such a handsome face look so frighteningly reprimanding?

"Can you please speak English?" he continued.

She could do without his harsh tone, but the request was acceptable. "A small structure of his intestine burst open, and the inner lining of his abdomen was infected."

She scrunched her nose as she remembered the offensive smell which had gushed into the operating room when they'd cut him open.

"We normally make a small incision to remove the appendix." She held her thumb and pointer finger about four inches apart. "The incision we made is much bigger because we needed to clean out his abdomen. He has a tube connected to a bulb in place to drain out the fluid. Depending on the amount of drainage he has overnight, we'll see if we can remove it tomorrow."

She dragged her gaze away from Akin's and focused on the friendliest-looking of the four. "We have him on pain medication and antibiotics. He's resting comfortably."

"Can we see him?" the friendly-looking one asked, with a crooked grin.

"Yes, but only for a short while."

"Thank you, Dr..." Akin looked down at her chest. Her hardening nipples didn't understand that he'd only searched for her nametag. "Djan."

"I'll show you the way."

Or she could direct them there so she'd be out of their presence. When had her body ever reacted to a man just looking at her before?

It must be the fatigue.

Akin had never experienced such a rush of lightheaded relief as when he saw Ishaq. How could a dark-skinned man look pale? It was a wonder his best friend hadn't died.

"I'm going to kick your ass, just as soon as the doctor gives the okay to do so. Why the hell did you wait so long? You're a damn doctor."

Ishaq's eyes crept open with a groan. "I'm on my deathbed, and you're yelling at me? What kind of brother are you?"

"One you scared the hell out of," Akin answered. "She said they had to gut you and clean out all of your shit, but you'll be fine."

Ishaq's smile was small, but present. A good sign. "I'm sure that's exactly how she expressed it."

"She left out the shit part," Dubem said. "But we knew what she meant."

Ishaq responded with a grunt as his eyes closed.

Akin took a moment to send up a gruff prayer of gratitude. God hadn't featured much in his life, but he couldn't deny His presence during times like this.

They stepped away from the bed to let their brother rest.

Dubem rubbed his hands together. "Now that I know he's okay, there's a fine honey I'd like to talk up."

Commander Dubem Nzeogwu had the reputation of getting any woman he lusted after with little more than a flash of his double dimples and a few sweet words. Did he want to make a play on Dr. Djan? Akin's short nails dug into the flesh of his palms.

They'd made it to the door when the soft patter of feet caught his attention. The woman who'd helped save Ishaq's life swept into the room with a nod and an antiseptic scent. She went to their comrade and spoke in soft tones Akin couldn't discern. He turned his full attention towards her, unable to keep his eyes from roaming along the lushness of a body that even a baggy light green uniform couldn't hide.

Dubem's low whistle made it to Akin's ears.

For the first time in a very long time, a deep stab of jealousy twisted in his gut, and he restrained himself from punching the pretty boy in the jaw. "Don't even try it."

Dubem's eyes narrowed for a flash. Akin got the impression that he'd been seen as a rival the man hadn't expected.

Dubem raised both hands up in defence and laughed, distilling the tension that had crept between them. "Fine."

Dr. Djan glanced in their direction. Akin's heart stilled for an incredible moment as their gazes met. Her obsidian eyes held his as he soaked in the flawlessness of her dark skin. The scar reaching upward from her eyebrow to the hairline intrigued him. What had caused it?

He'd probably never know.

The corners of her lips rose into a slight smile as she focused on her patient again. Yes, her beauty had captivated him, but the innate sorrow he'd witnessed in her irises tore at his spirit. Screaming at him to bring her peace. What could've happened in her life that had caused her eyes to be filled with such agony and despair? It had registered earlier, but he'd blamed the observation on his own anxiety.

"Akin," Dubem said.

"What?"

"They don't like it when you stare."

At the sound of Dubem's chuckle, Akin forced himself to look away to glare at his friend.

The laughter continued. "Just a bit of advice. With your *charming* personality, you'll need all the help you can get."

Akin knew the truth when he heard it. Unless the woman liked direct, forthright men who couldn't stay in one location to save his life, he had no chance.

OTHER BOOKS BY LOVE AFRICA PRESS

Healing His Medic by Nana Prah

Ere's Secret and 223 Bonny Street by Firi Kamson

Dawsk by Erhu Kome Yellow

Diary of a Wallflower by Glory Abah

Love and the Lawless Anthology by Emem Bassey, Onyeoma Izunna, Julie Onoh, Obinna Obioma and Kiru Taye

CONNECT WITH US

Facebook.com/LoveAfricaPress

Twitter.com/LoveAfricaPress

Instagram.com/LoveAfricaPress

www.loveafricapress.com